TO SAVE HIS LIFE

Also by Kelley Roos

WHO SAW MAGGIE BROWN?

ONE FALSE MOVE

CRY IN THE NIGHT

GRAVE DANGER

NECESSARY EVIL

REQUIEM FOR A BLONDE

THE BLONDE DIED DANCING

TO SAVE HIS LIFE

BY KELLEY ROOS

DODD, MEAD & COMPANY
NEW YORK

RED BADGE MYSTERY

Library of Congress Catalog Card Number: 68-26154

Printed in the United States of America
by Vail-Ballou Press, Inc., Binghamton, N. Y.

FOR JANE EAGER

TO SAVE HIS LIFE

CHAPTER I

THE CAR RACED south along the Spanish coast, a slim, dark streak in the moonlight. It followed the sudden twists of the rugged mountain road, then swooped down to the little cove town called Cala Brava. It slowed in the narrow streets of the village and came to a stop in the parking lot outside a hotel beside the sea. The young American slipped from under the steering wheel and stood for a moment looking at the small hotel, ablaze with light, throbbing with noise. He looked at it with gratitude. There would be a drink in there; he needed a drink. It had been a long day.

Diego, one of the bellboys, came running to meet him; he took the two cameras and the bag of photographic equipment from the back seat. He would put it, he said, in Señor's room. But first, he diplomatically inquired, had the Señor's mission been a success? The Señor assured him that it had been. He had taken many pictures of many lovely girls on the beach at Cadaqués. Readers of a certain American travel magazine would almost certainly be beguiled by them. While they might not ever visit Cadaqués, they might quite possibly renew their subscription to the magazine.

At the desk the clerk held mail in his extended hands.

"Good evening, Mr. Towers," he said. "You have returned. I am delighted."

"Pedro, you and Diego have grace. You will soon go to New York and be millionaires."

"Is that rich?"

"If you have the right tax man."

He looked at his mail. A check from a magazine for a picture story he had done on the ancient bullring in Frejus, two dunning letters from credit card concerns, his hotel bill. He paid the bill to Pedro, put the other letters in his pocket.

"Mr. Towers," Pedro said, "your friends are waiting for you in the bar."

"Where else?" he said.

He went into the bar; it was vastly overpopulated. Any tourist, American-born, American-bred, would have looked at once for an indignant and alarmed fireman counting its occupants. What he looked for was Enid, England's most gorgeous girl, and he saw her struggling through the thirsty mob to greet him. Following in her wake was Gerald Chapman, Enid's current playmate. Gerald, too, was English. He had fought the abortive, unsatisfactory battle of Suez and he had vowed that never again in his life would he do anything, anything at all. It was humiliating to do anything, he said; nothing turned out well anymore. Damn it all, he said.

"Larry, darling," Enid said.

"Miss England," he said.

"You keep calling me that," Enid said, smiling gratefully but sadly, "but I was never Miss England. But my mother, God rest her soul, was Miss British Empire. She was the last one. The sun sat on her."

"Larry, chum," Gerald said, "how was it in Cadaqués?"

"Thank you for asking."

"No," Enid said, "he is interested in how it was in Cadaqués for you. And so am I."

"It is possible," he said, "that I took splendid pictures. The light was right. The girls were lovely. The beaches looked their most enticing. I may make five hundred dollars American because I spent the day in Cadaqués."

"I am delighted," Gerald said, "that I encouraged you to go."

"Thank you," he said.

"Larry!" a French voice said.

Nicole, one of France's most beautiful young women, came out of the crowd and whispered, over her vodka on the rocks, into his ear. "Don't look at me, Larry, dear. My eyes are red. My face is swollen. I have been weeping all day. Tom is gone."

"Tom?" he said. "Tom has gone?"

"My eyes are red," Nicole said. "My face is swollen. My heart is heavy. Tom is on his way back to New York."

"Pardon me," an American voice said, "but my wife wants to know. Are you the international set?"

The four of them turned and regarded the small, embarrassed man. He lifted a hand to point across the barroom to a stout woman drinking a lemonade at a corner table. She was formidable; she evoked sympathy for the small husband she had sent on this errand.

"Are we the international set?" repeated Enid. "What a lovely question! You darling little bit of a man. Are we the international set?"

"No," Gerald said, "we are not. We are the jet set."

"Yes, come to think of it, that's what we are," Enid said.

"We are third-generation Fitzgerald, not second."

"Fitzgerald," the small husband said. "That's the name of a whiskey."

"Poor, dear Scott," Enid said. "But you are right. That is the name of a whiskey. Tell your wife that we are the international set and that we constantly drink Fitzgerald whiskey."

"Thank you," the husband said. "Like I said, she made me ask you."

They watched him struggle back through the crowded room to his large wife, and Enid said, "Poor, sweet little man. If my heart were in the right place, I would break up that marriage."

"May I remind you, love," Gerald said, "that you haven't quite yet broken up my marriage. One marriage at a time."

Nicole said, "Larry, I am so unhappy. I am desolate."

"Because Tom's on his way back to New York," he said. "Why did he go?"

Gerald answered. "Counted his money at lunch."

"Depressing sight," Enid said.

"It was then I began to weep," Nicole said.

"Holiday all over for Tom," Gerald said. "Back to the money-grubbing grind. Without delay. He had just about enough left for air fare. Took off for Barcelona by bus, poor lad. He was able to pick up a cancellation on Iberia for New York. Leaving at midnight. What do you think we should do, Larry?"

"The least we can do," he said, "is see him off."

"We have been discussing that, Enid and I," Gerald said. "We must see Tom off, least we can do."

"We'll have to hurry," Nicole said. "It is late; we can just make it."

"Nicole, dear," Enid said, "can you really bear to say good-by to Tom again? Need you torture yourself more? We will drop you off at your place."

"Yes," Nicole said, "that would be merciful of you. One should not say good-by twice. You are right. One should not torture oneself. But, Larry, you will have a drink with me and we will toast Tom, yes?"

"Yes," he said.

They took care of that while his car was brought back out of the parking lot. There was a brief discussion about who should drive. Gerald said that he should, because Larry had been driving for hours. Nicole pointed out that Larry had had only one drink; Gerald had had quite a few too many. Enid slipped behind the steering wheel and said, "Get in, I'm driving."

"Oh, God, no," Gerald said.

"I am not tired," Enid said, "and I have had nothing to drink since lunchtime. Then, too, I am a wonderful driver."

"That's it," Gerald said, groaning. "Beware of a driver who is proud of his driving."

Enid started the motor, put the car in gear. Gerald got in beside her, the other two piled into the back seat. Gerald made sure that everyone had fastened his safety belt and the car took off. Behind the wheel Enid lost all the allure of her sex; she drove like a man racing for money. When Gerald reminded her that the Romans had built this road for men on foot and horseback and not for insane motorists, she laughed at him and stepped harder on the gas pedal.

In the rear seat of the open Jaguar the wind was a gale. "Larry," Nicole said, and he had to bend his ear to her lips to hear what she was saying. "Larry, speak to me of Tom," she said, "tell me about him. You were boys together."

"Well, not quite," he said. "We met in college."

"And the girls," Nicole said, "they were mad for him, yes?"

"They were mad for him, yes."

"Did he have a special one at this school?"

"No," he said. "Tom played the field."

"Played the field?" Nicole said.

"There was no special girl that I remember," he said.

"I see," Nicole said plaintively. "There were many special girls, yes? Do you think you could light me a cigarette, Larry? I need the comfort of a cigarette."

"I can try," he said.

He took a cigarette from the breast pocket of his jacket. His lighter was in his trouser pocket. He had to undo his safety belt to get at it. Then, when he was leaning forward, using the front seats as a shield to light the cigarette that was to comfort Nicole, he heard the tire beneath him explode. He felt the car swerve and careen off the embankment on the inside of the road. Nicole screamed. Gerald cursed and fought with Enid for the steering wheel. The car smashed into the low stone guard at the cliff's edge and it rose into space.

"Larry!" Nicole shrieked, and reached out for him. But he felt himself lifted out of the seat, out of the car and hurled clear of it.

It was a second, less than a second, before he struggled to his hands and knees and crawled to the brink of the precipice. Below him, so far below that the car seemed to be a miniature, he saw its wild plunge halted by a stand of great boulders. Then they released it and it rolled over and over, slowly and gently, bursting into flames. Then it lay still, burning brightly, turning the sea beside it into an orange glow.

CHAPTER 2

FOR MORE THAN an hour now he had been wandering around Times Square, watching it, but without interest, fill up to overflowing with tourists, native pleasure seekers, the night people. This was the fourth round trip he had made up Seventh Avenue to Fifty-seventh Street, down Broadway, back into the Square. He was delaying dinner, killing time; it was going to be a long evening. He knew he should go to the theater, see a play or a picture, but he couldn't bring himself around to doing it. Turning into a side street, he looked for a relatively quiet bar where he would have another drink before he had dinner, and that was all he would have. Drinking wasn't helping. Besides, he had to be in shape, clear-minded and fairly quick-witted, for his appointment tomorrow with a Miss Lisa Martin, an associate editor of the magazine *World Travel.*

In a place, relatively quiet, called Orlando's, he cunningly ordered a beer; three beers would approximate one whiskey alcoholically and take more than three times as long to drink. Behind him a delighted soprano voice said, "Vic!

Hello, Vic Jacoby!"

In the bar mirror he saw, behind his left shoulder, the reflection of a mop of genuine honey-colored hair. He lowered his left shoulder as far as he could and saw a pair of wide blue eyes and an absolutely charming nose. The hair, the eyes and the nose all matched the gamin quality of the voice and for a moment he thought those eyes and his were connected in the mirror. Then he glanced to his right and to his left for this man Vic Jacoby, wondering why the idiot didn't respond to such a darling of a girl who was so delighted to see him again.

He felt, to his amazement, the touch of the darling girl's hand on his elbow. "Vic," she said, "you're not paying attention! Come to! Look who's here! It's me."

He swiveled on the bar stool, slid off it to his feet, and looked down into her face. The rest of it was no disappointment. The wide, smiling mouth, the strong but not too pugnacious chin were a photographer's dream come true. There were very few faces around like this one.

He said sincerely, "I'm sorry, but . . ."

The lips stopped smiling, the light went out of the merry eyes. "Vic," she said, "don't do this to me, please! Or are you kidding?"

"Believe me," he said, "I'm sorry that I'm not your friend Vic. My name is Larry Towers."

"All right," she said, and she smiled. But the lilt had gone out of her voice. "Okay, if that's the way you want it to be."

"Wait!" Larry said. "Look at me, take a better look at me! I can't be an absolute double for your friend."

Solemnly she regarded him, inspected him minutely, then she shook her head and her lips twisted into a rueful smile.

"It's fantastic how much you look like Vic; it's amazing. You are absolute doubles, except for one thing. Vic is taller than you."

"Vic must be pretty damn tall."

"Oh, yes, lovely tall. He . . . oh, dear, this is awfully embarrassing. Please forgive me!"

"Well," Larry said, "it was a God-awful thing for you to do, but if you'll let me buy you a drink, I'll consider forgiving you."

Before she could answer, a young man who had just stepped out of a phone booth opposite the bar was making his way toward the girl and she called to him, "How's Tony?"

"Bad news, dear," the young man said. "Tony's fine."

The girl sighed. "And Sandy?"

"And Sandy, unfortunately, is also in fine fettle. I told Ernie where we would be; let's go there."

"All right." She linked her arm into the young man's, then turned back to Larry and laughed. "If you and Vic should ever meet, you're both in for the shock of your lives."

"What's all this about?" the man said.

She smiled at him and said, "We'd better go. I'll tell you on the way."

As they hustled out of the bar, the girl looked over her shoulder and waved a humorous, apologetic good-by to Larry. He returned to his bar stool and his beer, peering into the mirror above the bar to see what Vic Jacoby looked like.

Lisa Martin, associate editor of *World Travel*, was in her mid-thirties, smart but not chic, feminine but not soft. The new breed of career girl, Larry thought, as she made it clear that she was buying the lunch and they would have no nonsense about that. She ordered straight gin on the rocks, he ordered bourbon and soda. When he offered her a cigarette, she refused and insisted that he try one of her super-king-sized filtertips out of the super-king-sized filtertip silver cigarette case that Tiffany's must have hastily made. Larry didn't feel that he could refuse her, but the cigarette definitely wasn't worthy of its case.

"I needn't tell you," Lisa Martin was telling him, "how much we like your work."

"Well, you like enough of it."

"Most of it," Lisa said. "Nobody else around right now has a better batting average with us than you. Do you have some ideas for more stories?"

"At the moment, no. I was hoping that you might have some."

"We just might," Lisa said. "How about the new royal colony they're setting up in Marbella? A story of the Windsors and their friends there?"

Larry took a drag on the cigarette, then said, "I would rather not go back to Spain for a while."

Lisa looked at him for a moment, then she said, "I won't ask you why."

"There was an automobile accident," Larry said. "Three friends of mine were killed. I was in the car with them." He crushed the cigarette in the crystal ash tray at his place. "You know, this is the first time I've ever been in New York. Except for an hour or two once at Kennedy Airport."

Lisa smiled. "You sound surprised about that, and I can see why. You must have been in almost every other big city in the world. How did you happen to miss New York? The biggest city in your own country."

"That's right. Funny, isn't it?"

"You're a California boy, I know. And that is exactly all I know about you."

"I'm San Francisco."

"Lucky you. I suppose you went to school at Berkeley? Or was it Stanford?"

"It was Berkeley," Larry said, "but only for two years. Then I bummed around for a while and ended up in Chicago, taking pictures of ketchup and mustard for an advertising agency there."

"And that's what drove you out of your native land without ever seeing New York."

Larry laughed and said, "The reason I mentioned that this was my first time here. I thought maybe I could do a picture story about New York. Give it the same treatment I give the cities over there."

"An American discovers New York?" Lisa said. "It's a strange, foreign place to him, exotic and all that."

Larry nodded. "Yes. Don't spoil the natives."

"That might be fun."

They discussed that idea through lunch and into coffee, just coffee, black, no dessert. While they were considering a possible piece with a Mexico City background, the waiter brought a note to the table.

"A lady asked me to give this to you, sir."

Larry unfolded the slip of paper. *Dear Vic,* it said. *I wouldn't dream of breaking up your tête-à-tête, but why don't you meet me for a drink tonight at Starr's, just off Fifth on West Fifty-third? I'll be waiting for you at the bar. Nine o'clock. Dying to see you again. Love, Polly G.*

Larry beckoned to the waiter and he came back to their table.

"Where is the lady?" Larry asked.

"She's gone now, sir. She gave me that just as she was leaving."

Larry laughed and shook his head.

"What is it?" Lisa asked.

Larry handed her the note, then told her what had happened to him the night before.

"You must really look like this Vic Jacoby," Lisa said. "I wonder who he is."

"I have no idea," Larry said. "All I know is that he isn't listed in the phone book. I was curious. I looked him up."

"Are you going to keep this date with Polly G?"

"I think I'd better. I can't let poor Polly stand there at the bar, thinking unkind thoughts about Vic. I'll stop in and explain to her. It's the least I can do for Vic."

As he walked down the length of the long and busy bar, a stout, pleasant-faced woman somewhere in her fifties stepped into Larry's path. She beamed at him, she extended both plump hands toward him. She was even more pleased to see him than the girl last night had been.

"Vic," she said, "how are you? You're certainly looking fine! Where did you get that gorgeous tan? Where have you been?"

Larry gently rescued his hands from her clasp and said, "I'm sorry to disappoint you, but I'm not Vic Jacoby. My name is Towers, Larry Towers."

"Vic!" Still beaming, she shook a finger at him. "It isn't nice to tease old ladies!"

"I'm not joking, I . . ."

She burst into a hearty laugh that made her broad shoulders shake and her plentiful bosom bounce. "Are you on the lam, Vic? Did you rob a bank?"

"Do you want to see my driver's license?"

She quieted down and peered intently up into his face. "You are serious, aren't you?" she said. "My God, I can't believe it! You and Vic are identical twins; it's incredible!"

"I believe it," Larry said. "This is the first time I've ever been in New York, and I've only been here three days. But you're the second person to mistake me for this Vic Jacoby. Who is he? What does he do? Where does he live? Suppose you let me buy you a drink and you tell me about him."

"I've ordered you a drink," Polly said. "Or rather, I've ordered a rye and soda for Vic. Vic likes rye and soda."

"I'll drink Vic's rye and soda, thank you, Miss G. Or is it Mrs. G?"

"It's Mrs. Grant, but please call me Polly. All the boys do, all of Freddy's friends. Vic Jacoby is a friend of my son Freddy."

Mrs. Polly Grant had resettled herself on her bar stool. She rode it as though born to it, and she sipped her drink with enthusiasm, but with a control that bespoke vast experience. Her bag, gloves, cigarettes, lighter, folded newspaper overflowed into the domain of the gentleman drinking beer at her left, but Larry noticed that he didn't seem to mind. Cheerful and bland-faced, he seemed to be amused by her.

"Actually," Polly Grant was saying, "I've only seen Vic a half dozen times or so, and I don't know him all that well. It was really because of Freddy that I sent you that note. Freddy has lost touch with Vic during the past year or two, but he's always wondering whatever happened to him. I know he'd just love to see him again. I was hoping I could get Vic to drive up to Larchmont with me tonight and surprise Freddy."

"Tell me something about Vic," Larry said. "How does he make a living?"

"Oh, heavens, I wouldn't have any idea! That's one thing I never heard Vic and Freddy discuss, anything as dull as how to make a living. No, with those two it was all fun and games."

"Where did Vic live?"

"I don't know that, either. Someplace in Manhattan though, I'm pretty sure."

"You wouldn't happen to remember the names of any of his girls, would you?"

"No, I don't, but Freddy would, of course. Say, Larry!"

"Yes, Polly?"

"I wonder," she said, tilting her head, eyeing him closely, "if you've got Vic's sense of humor as well as his looks. Could you go along with a gag?"

"I might," he said, doubtful about Vic Jacoby's sense of humor. "Try me."

"You busy tonight?"

"No."

"Suppose," she said, her chuckle rising into a rolling laugh that she talked through, "I drive us up to see Freddy and Milly. Oh, I forgot, you wouldn't know . . . Milly is Freddy's wife. And you be Vic! See how long you can keep them fooled!"

"Oh, I don't think so, Polly," he said. "I don't believe that I . . ."

"Oh, come on, Larry," she pleaded. "Be a sport!"

He looked down into her plump face, glowing with eagerness and high spirits. She made him feel like a stuffed shirt, like an adult refusing to let a child go out trick or treating on Hallowe'en. What the hell, he thought, why not go along with her gag? He had nothing to lose except another evening alone.

"You haven't noticed yet, Polly, but I'm not as tall as Vic Jacoby."

"So get up on your toes a little!" she said. "Sit down right away! Come on!"

Her car was parked in the garage next door and while Larry paid the check she brought the Plymouth sedan to the front of the bar where he was waiting. In the city she drove cautiously, even a little nervously, as though she had learned to drive late in life, but once they were off Bruckner Boulevard and on the thruway she relaxed. Soon she had him talking about himself. He told her his parents had died before he was eleven and he had been raised by an aunt in San Francisco. He told her how he had dropped out of Berkeley, bummed around for a while, tried a job in Chicago for a while and, finally, how he had gone abroad as a free-lance photographer and travel writer.

She was such a good listener, so interested and sympathetic, that he even found himself telling her about Enid and Gerald, Nicole and Tom, and about the night they were on their way to see Tom off at Barcelona. Except for his brief mention of the accident to Lisa Martin, this was the first time he had spoken of it since he had made his report to the Spanish police. It did him good; somehow that night, so vivid and sharp to him, seemed to fade a little into the past. It no longer seemed possible that it had happened less than a week ago.

After that they rode in silence for a while, then she was telling him obviously oft-told tales of her life, and they were soon laughing together again. Mother Grant, it seemed, had not lived an orderly, quiet, motherly life. As she warmed to her stories, they became too tall and funny and ribald to be completely true. She was overdoing, Larry realized, in order to entertain him, to make him forget what had happened on the road to Barcelona. He began to look forward to meeting Freddy. He was glad now that he was going along with her gag.

The Plymouth turned off the thruway into the town of Larchmont and onto a countrylike road beyond it. Mrs. Grant explained that Freddy kept a horse for himself, one for Milly, so their house was quite a way out of town, on ten acres of pretty, rolling meadow land. The headlights, Larry noticed, were picking out fewer and fewer roadside homes, the spaces between them widened. Twice he saw final windows darken; it was bedtime in suburbia. Suddenly the motor sputtered, then conked out, and the car rolled to a stop.

"Oh, dear," Polly Grant said, "I think I must be out of gas. I can't remember when I last bought any."

Larry leaned toward the dashboard. "Your gauge says almost a quarter full."

"Oh, dear," Polly said ruefully, "my gauge is broken. It's been broken for months. Isn't that like me?"

Larry laughed and said, "Have you got a flashlight?"

"In the glove compartment, but it can't possibly work. I seem to remember writing batteries on a list not very long ago."

Larry found the flashlight in the glove compartment; it was weak but it worked. He went to the back of the car and, training the flash on the gas tank flap, he tipped it open. He had only touched the cap to unscrew it when he heard the Plymouth's motor start up. Then, with the thrust of a jet, it took off. It streaked down the road, its motor roaring, and Larry stood, stunned, and watched the taillights disappear around a curve. He was aware then of a car coming from behind him, coming fast, its headlights washing over him. He leaped back off the road and he heard the crack of a gun shot, felt the flashlight fall from his hand.

Instinctively, with no thought or wonder, he dove deeper off the road; rolling and scrambling, he pushed his way into the underbrush. He heard the car slow down and screech to a stop. Then it went into reverse and he could hear it coming back toward him.

On his belly he wormed his way into the tangled undergrowth until his hands touched a low stone wall. He heard gun shots as he swarmed it. Crouching low, he ran in the shadow of the wall, using it as a shield. But the driver of the car had heard him stumbling through the brush; the car was moving parallel to him, moving at the same speed. Turning, he fled in the opposite direction. He found an opening in the brush and ran through it to a field, away from the highway.

CHAPTER 3

IT WAS NEARING midnight when Larry walked down Lexington Avenue toward his hotel. His jacket and trousers had been torn in several places in his scramble through the brush. He felt no ill will toward the brush; it had saved his life. Someday, he thought, he must go back and pay it a little homage. During the next dry spell he might water it—if he lived that long. If he didn't stop looking like Vic Jacoby.

He had worked his way back to the highway, hiding in that admirable brush each time a car had appeared, no matter what direction it appeared from. All he knew about the gunmen's car was that it was a sedan, so he waited until a truck came by. There was a car tailing close behind the first truck that passed him; he didn't flag it; he hid. It was a long time before a truck passed when there was no other vehicle in sight. When the driver stopped and he climbed into the cab, he knew for sure that he was not being followed. The gunmen had given up for the moment, at least, or he had shaken them. The truck started moving.

"What's your trouble, buddy?" the driver asked.

There seemed no point in telling the truth. "My car conked out," Larry said.

"I didn't see any car."

"It's up a side road back there."

"You want me to take you to a garage?"

"No, I've got to get to New York."

"I'm going as far as the Bronx."

"Thanks."

"What about your car?"

"I'll do something about it tomorrow."

It had been two hours, maybe three, since the woman called Polly Grant had left him stranded on a lonely country road and gunmen in a car that was following hers had fired on him. But he was still stunned and dazed by what had happened; he still had to tell himself that it was no nightmare, no trip gone wrong; it had happened.

The most incredible part of it all was the woman. He had sat beside her in the bar, had talked to her face to face, but he hadn't been able to convince her that he was not Vic Jacoby. She had pretended to believe him, then she had conned him into taking a ride into a death trap. In the car she had let him tell the story of his life, had clucked her sympathy and tried to cheer him, and not for one second had she believed one word he said. She had driven him merrily along into the trap.

The truck driver had let him out in the Bronx and he had taken a subway into Manhattan, got off at Fifty-ninth Street. His hotel was a five-minute walk from the stop.

He was about to turn off Lexington into Fifty-third Street when he saw the man standing on the opposite corner, thirty feet from the hotel's only entrance, and the sight of him made Larry duck into the nearest doorway. He had seen that man before, recently, here in New York. When and where was it? He had seen the bland and affable face reflected in a mirror. Was it in the bar last night when the girl had mistaken him for Vic Jacoby? No, he knew that wasn't it, and then he had it. This man had been sitting at the bar this evening, next to Polly Grant, had seemed faintly amused by her. It could hardly be a coincidence that a few hours later he would be loitering outside his hotel.

He felt sure that the man had not yet seen him. Darting out of the doorway, he walked quickly, but not too quickly, back up Lexington Avenue, hugging the line of the buildings. He cursed himself for the idiot he was, for thinking that he had shaken the gunmen, for never considering that they might know where he lived. But he had needed time to think, and he had needed a drink. He had thought he could satisfy both those needs in his hotel room while he packed and made plans to get out of there. Now he realized he needed help, and immediately.

Detective Lieutenant Corso's desk was in a corner of the squad room, the quietest corner in honor of Corso's long service on the force. Larry wasn't always certain as he told him his story that the detective was giving him his undivided attention. He wasn't sure, either, if the detective was believing his story. Finally he said, "Do you think I'm a nut, a crank? That I dreamed this up?"

"No," Corso said, "you don't look like a nut to me. You look like a guy that's been shot at with intent to kill."

"Thanks!"

"Take it easy," Corso said, "as easy as possible. That's quite a line-up that's out to get this Jacoby, a real team effort. There's this Mrs. Grant, and you think there were two men in the car."

"At least two," Larry said. "The shots came from the right-hand side, not from the driver's side. And the man waiting outside my hotel might have been in the car, or he could be a third man."

"Whichever," Corso said, "he might still be waiting for you on the corner there. Let's go see."

In the detective's small black sedan they cruised three times around the hotel. The man Larry had seen was gone. Corso said he would like a sandwich and a glass of milk and maybe Larry would be interested in joining him while they decided what to do about all this. Larry said maybe Corso could have his sandwich and milk someplace where a man who needed a drink could get one. A few minutes later they were giving their orders to a chubby waitress in a restaurant-bar on Third Avenue.

"Your coat's torn," the waitress said to Larry. "You need a woman to look after you."

"I need more than a woman to look after me," he said.

"Whatever that's supposed to mean," the waitress said, and went away.

"I suppose," Corso said, "you'll be wanting a twenty-four-hour-a-day bodyguard."

"For the rest of my life?"

"It might not be long," Corso said. "If they're sincere, a bodyguard might not stop them for long."

"That's right," Larry said. "I think I've got a better idea."

"Like you got to get lost and give up looking like this Jacoby?"

"Yes," Larry said, "while you find this Jacoby, find out who is trying to kill him, and take care of them."

"Good thinking," Corso said, "for a man that was being

shot at only a couple of hours ago. I been shot at off and on in the past thirty years. Uncomfortable, isn't it?"

"It's no way to live," Larry said.

"No, it isn't," Corso said. "Yeah, we got to find this Jacoby. This girl the other night who knew him . . . you didn't get her name?"

"No."

"She didn't tell you anything about Jacoby that would help?"

"She told me nothing about Jacoby. Only that he's taller than I am."

"You're no midget," Corso said, "but there's quite a few around taller than you. So that doesn't help. And everything this Mrs. Grant told you about Jacoby is a pack of lies, of course."

Larry nodded. "Maybe," he said, "Jacoby has a police record."

"I'll go into all that. I'll take care of locating Jacoby. What about you? You'll check into another hotel?"

"That's right."

"What about your things? Want me to get them out for you?"

Larry frowned. "No. Leave them there."

"You afraid somebody would spot us taking them?"

"I think it's possible. Don't you?"

Corso nodded. "Sure, it's possible. If there's enough of them looking for you, it's even likely." The waitress made her delivery. Larry knocked back half of his double bourbon while the detective was reaching for the mustard. Then Corso said, "Okay, you take care of getting yourself lost and not looking like Jacoby. We'll try to take care of the rest."

By ten o'clock the next morning he was pretty well set. In a secondhand store on Second Avenue he had bought a cheap suitcase. In a thrift shop on the other side of the street he got a pair of not-too-used slacks, a black turtle-neck sweater, a jacket whose cuffs were frayed only a little, and a slouch hat. He bought dark glasses in a five and ten. Then he checked into an obscure and inexpensive hotel just off Union Square.

He waited until late afternoon to phone Corso. So far it appeared that Jacoby had no criminal record, at least not in New York. They were checking other cities, other states. So far they had not been able to locate the girl through Orlando's Bar. So far they were at a dead end but, Corso said, it was still early.

For the next week he telephoned the precinct twice a day for a progress report. He always hung up frustrated and disappointed. They had discovered no police record anywhere for Vic Jacoby. They had gone through all the approved methods of tracing a missing person with a constant lack of success. Using Larry's meager description of the girl in Orlando's, they had tried to find her. Unfortunately, there were too many blonde girls with wide blue eyes and a nose that could be described as charming, a word that made the practical Corso groan.

At the end of the week Larry gave up. He spent the next two weeks holed up in his dreary room, devoting twenty-four hours a day, channeling all his energy into growing a beard.

At the end of that time he surveyed himself in the cracked full-length mirror that hung on the back of his closet door. He saw a six-foot bearded man, wearing used but not shabby clothes, dark glasses and a hat. He no longer looked like

Larry Towers; therefore, he reasoned, he no longer looked like Vic Jacoby. He looked like a hundred thousand young men wearing a beard and dark glasses and a hat. Now he felt safe enough to venture into midtown Manhattan and see if he could do what the police could not—find Vic Jacoby.

He knew that his best chance of doing that was to locate the girl in Orlando's Bar. Of course his description of her to the police had been worthless. Furthermore, it was possible that only that one time had she ever been in the place. But, hoping against hope, he found Orlando's and for the next several nights spent hours there, a tall, quiet, bearded man who sat drinking his beer slowly and watching.

There came at last the time when he knew it was no go. It seemed certain that the girl and her escort had stopped into the bar that one night because they had need of a telephone. She would never come there again. He paid for what he decided would be his last drink at Orlando's.

He drifted around Times Square, still looking into the face of every young blonde girl in sight. It had become a habit now. On Forty-fourth Street the three theater marquees were alight; it was after eight o'clock, nearing curtain time. He considered going to a play. For weeks now he had done nothing but brood about Vic Jacoby, his blonde friend in Orlando's, Mrs. Polly Grant and her lethal colleagues. He couldn't spend the rest of his life doing that. It would be interesting, he thought, to see if a play could take his mind off his problem.

He stopped in front of the next theater and read a billboard. It told him that Antoinette James and Alexander Terry were the stars of a brand-new comedy, *Where There's Smoke*. In the lobby he looked at photographs of the two actors. Miss James was a raven-haired beauty. Mr. Terry was an aging leading man, a little too handsome. Neither name meant anything to him; he would see what else Forty-fifth Street had to offer. Back on the sidewalk, he took a few steps, then stopped, turned and looked up at the blazing marquee.

ANTOINETTE JAMES AND ALEXANDER TERRY
IN
WHERE THERE'S SMOKE

But those two names, he realized, did mean something to him. Not because they were the leading players in a new Broadway hit. It was something else—something that had happened since he had been in New York, and now he remembered.

He had been talking to the blonde girl in Orlando's. A young man had stepped out of the phone booth and she had said to him, *How's Tony?* He had answered that the news was bad, Tony was fine. *How's Sandy?* she had asked, and he had said that unfortunately Sandy was fine, too. He had told someone where they would be; he suggested that they go there.

Larry took a deep breath. Could he be right? Good Lord, let him be right, for his own sake, for Vic Jacoby's sake. Tony and Sandy could be nicknames for Antoinette and Alexander. The blonde girl and the young man might have been rueful over their good health because it meant that the two stars would play the performance that night. Someone had told where they were going. That might have been in case one of the stars became incapacitated during the performance. The blonde girl could be Antoinette James' understudy.

His first thought was to inquire at the box office, but the lobby was jammed, the box office people busy. He found the alley leading to the stage door. The stage doorman, surprisingly youthful, only in his late fifties, asked him his business.

"I'd like to see Miss James' understudy, please."

"You don't know her name?" the doorman said.

"No, it happens I don't."

"How come you want to see somebody you don't know the name?"

"Look, this is very important."

"And look, this is why theaters have stage doormen. To protect the people back here."

"Is the producer here?"

"We got four producers. You'd think one of them would happen to be here, but no, they got a hit. They're somewheres or other spending money."

"Can I speak to the stage manager?" Larry asked.

"He's busy."

Larry showed the doorman a five-dollar bill.

"He's still busy."

He showed him another five dollars. The doorman extended a practiced hand, took the money and hid it in his pants. He turned, leaned through a doorway behind him and yelled, "Hey, Charley, a fella asking for you!"

It took Charley a few minutes to show up. He was a burly young man, pleasant.

"Sorry to keep you waiting," he said. "I was checking the prop list."

Larry didn't ask him if the prop list had checked out all right. "My name is Towers," he said. "Larry Towers. Do you by any chance happen to read *World Travel?*"

"I can't say I do," Charley said.

"I never miss it," the doorman said. "I never been out of New York and I never will. I get my kicks out of *World Travel*, *Holiday* and the *National Geographic*. Larry Towers, yeah, you did a thing lately about Gibraltar."

"That's right," Larry said. "Now I'd like to do a theater piece about understudies. I'd like to start with Miss James' understudy. I thought maybe you would help me get in touch with her."

"Actually," Charley said, "Midge isn't an understudy; she's a stand-by. Understudies usually play small parts and are always around when we need them. In a show like this, with no small parts, we hire damn good actors to cover the leads. They don't have to come to the theater unless they're going to play. They just tell us where they are in case we need them."

"So Midge isn't here now," Larry said. "What's her last name?"

"Redding," Charley said. "No, she's spending the evening at home." He laughed. "That isn't like Midge."

Larry said, "Would you give me her phone number? I'd like to make an appointment with her if she's interested."

It was quite awhile before the phone was answered. "Hello," a sleepy voice said.

"Miss Redding?" Larry said.

"Mmmm," she said.

"I woke you up."

"I was reading and watching television and I fell asleep and I dreamed that I was reading and watching television. Who is this?"

"You're a busy girl," he said. "This is Larry Towers. About a month ago at a bar called Orlando's you mistook me for . . ."

"Vic Jacoby," she said. "I remember your first name was Larry, but I didn't remember your last name." Her voice came wide awake. "I didn't tell you my name, did I? How did you find me? Why are you calling?"

"I want to get in touch with Vic Jacoby."

"Sorry, but I have no idea where he is. I don't even know if he's in New York."

"Could you give me the name of anyone who might know?"

"No, I don't think I know anyone."

"This is really serious," Larry said. "Vic Jacoby is in trouble. Bad trouble. Could I come to see you? Right away? Maybe you'll think of some way I can get to Jacoby."

"615 East Forty-ninth Street," she said. "Apartment 9-B."

"I can be there in about fifteen minutes," he said.

Her building was as close to the East River as a building could get. It featured studio apartments, one-room arrangements for working girls, and it did not trust heaven to protect them. There was a doorman; there was television in the elevators so that the doorman could keep his eye on his charges from their rooms to the lobby and back again. Larry told the man on duty that Miss Redding was expecting him. The man confirmed that.

"Ninth floor," he said. "Second door to the right, apartment 9-B."

"Thank you," Larry said.

When he rang the bell of 9-B, its door swung open almost immediately, then it was immediately slammed shut in his face. He realized that he had forgotten to tell Midge about his face. The door opened again, but only as far as the chain would permit.

"Who are you?" Midge said. "Go away!"

"Larry Towers," he said. He took off his hat and the dark glasses. "Sorry I forgot to mention the beard on the phone."

"My God, what are you made up for?"

"May I come in? And explain?"

"Yes!"

He told her what had happened to him. He told her about Mrs. Grant, the lovable Polly, and her gunmen, and that they were trying to kill him because they thought he was Vic Jacoby. He asked her to help him find Jacoby to warn him of his danger. And, incidentally, to save his own life.

CHAPTER 4

"DO YOU KNOW anyone," Larry said, "who might know where Vic Jacoby is?"

Midge shook her head.

"You mean," Larry said, "that you never met any of his friends?"

"That seems strange, doesn't it?"

"Yes," Larry said. "You look like the kind of a girl a guy would introduce to all his friends."

"Hey, thanks," Midge said. "That's the sort of thing a girl likes to hear."

"Obviously," Larry said, "Jacoby was the jealous type. He kept you to himself."

"I guess," Midge said, "I'd better tell you all about Vic and me."

"I guess so, if you don't mind."

"I do mind, really. I've never told anyone, but . . ."

"But under the circumstances?"

"Yes," Midge said. "Under the circumstances. I fell in love with Vic Jacoby at first sight. You know about Bennington?"

"A college for unusual girls. Somewhere in Vermont."

Midge nodded yes. "And after Christmas vacation they have this work period for the kids. You get a job someplace, you get experience. In my senior year I got a job doing research and taking dictation for an old actor who was writing a book about Eugene O'Neill and the Theatre Guild and himself. Mostly about himself. I lived at the Evangeline House, a Salvation Army sleep-in on Fourteenth Street. Reasonable rates, no men or dogs allowed."

"When was this?"

"Three years ago next Christmas."

"And you fell in love with Vic Jacoby at first sight."

"It couldn't have mattered less to him," Midge said. "Late afternoons, evenings, I used to go to the coffeehouses down under Washington Square in the Village. It happened like in *South Pacific*. You know, the 'Across a Crowded Room' bit. There was Vic. Here was I. Our eyes met. I smiled. He smiled. He came across the room to me. Only it turned out he wasn't smiling at me. He was laughing at me. He said I was the definitive hippy, and I guess I was. Hair down to my waist, pants or mini skirts, bare feet, weather permitting. Sandals when it didn't. I wasn't really the definitive hippy though, not really. I was a sissy about smoking pot."

"Was Vic making the scene? Pot and all?"

"No, no pot, not even a beard." She examined Larry and smiled. "Vic would have looked great in a beard."

"Thank you."

"And some people are really trying to kill Vic," she said slowly, incredulously. "You did tell me that five minutes ago, didn't you? You sat right there and told me that."

"They're not trying to kill Vic yet," Larry said. "They're trying to kill me. What was Vic doing in those days three years ago? Where did he work? How did he make a living?"

She shook her head. "I wouldn't know. We never talked about anything serious."

"He never mentioned any family? Didn't he ever tell you where he came from?"

"No, not that I remember. And I bet I remember everything Vic ever told me."

"And he didn't have any friends?" Larry said. "What kind of a guy was he, anyway?"

"He was the kind of a guy who would have lots and lots of friends!" Midge's voice rose in protest at Larry's derogatory questioning of Vic Jacoby's character. "I guess I haven't made it clear to you about Vic and me yet. I was never part of his personal life. I was just the little nut who went looking for him in the coffee houses and the bars. There was always a crowd around Vic, and never the same crowd. It was the scene, man!"

"And Jacoby was there, but he wasn't with it. What was he doing there?"

"He thought it was funny. Like he thought I was funny. But all this only lasted a couple of months. He stopped coming around before I went back to school in the spring."

"And you never saw him again," Larry said. "There goes the ball game. We aren't getting anyplace."

"I saw Vic once again," Midge said.

"Where? Here in New York?"

"No," Midge said. "It was abroad. In France."

"In France?" he said. "When?"

"Last summer. In August. The end of August, to be exact. To be very exact, it was a Friday."

"I was in France last summer," Larry said. "In France as

well as some other places. But, what the hell, so were a million other Americans. Tell me about it, Midge."

"Well, I'd had a year on the road in *Barefoot in the Park* and I was already signed to be Tony James' stand-by in this play, so I could afford a big-deal vacation. Paris, the Riviera, Florence, Rome. It was on a beach in France that I saw Vic. I came out of the water and there he was, sitting at a table with some people."

"It's going to turn out," Larry said, "that he kept on sitting with the people. You didn't get with him."

"No," Midge said, "we spent a little while together. An hour, maybe."

"You spent an hour alone with Vic Jacoby?"

"Yes," she said. She smiled ruefully. "Alone at last."

"And you talked to each other. He must have told you something about himself, what he was doing there, something. Try to remember."

"Sorry," Midge said, and this time her smile was embarrassed. "I'm afraid we talked mostly about me. I mean I talked mostly about me. He wanted to know what I'd been doing the last couple of years. And I was only too glad to tell him. Poor Vic."

"But you must have asked him something about himself! What he was doing in France, how long he was going to stay, what *he'd* been doing in the last couple of years. You were interested in the guy, for God's sake! You were in love with him!"

"When I did ask him questions about himself," Midge said, "he didn't give me any answers. He made jokes."

"Why? Do you think he was hiding something? Why was he such a man of mystery, for God's sake!"

"No, he wasn't that," Midge said firmly. "It's hard for me,

the definitive extrovert, to believe it, but there are people who don't like to talk about themselves. Vic was one of them. Or maybe," she said, frowning, "he just wasn't interested enough in me to tell me anything about himself."

"Do you think he was hanging around the Riviera the way he hung around the Village? A scene watcher?"

"You make him sound like a dope!" she said indignantly.

"Look at it this way," Larry said. "Because Vic Jacoby isn't available, he isn't around where they can shoot at him, they are shooting at me! That sort of thing doesn't endear my type to a man."

"But you are trying to save his life," Midge pointed out.

"I'm trying to save my own life," Larry said. "If his gets saved too, I'll let him have it, but mainly I want the police to catch these people who are shooting at me and take their guns away from them. I want to shave off this beard and look the way I look and go on my way. Midge, there must be something you know about Jacoby that would help!. Think, please think!"

She got up and walked slow circles around the room, her forehead crinkled. Occasionally she tapped her temples in frustration; almost constantly she ran her hands through her hair until it looked like a mop. The most attractive honey-colored mop within miles, Larry conceded, but still a mop. Suddenly she stopped pacing and stamped her feet in exasperation.

"I'm not thinking!" she shouted. "Not at all! I don't know where to begin! Everything is just a big blur!"

"Relax," Larry said. "Throw your mind back. Remember the Village three years ago . . . you used to see Vic Jacoby now and then . . . sometime or other he said something about where he came from or where he went to school, or something about a brother in Boston or . . ."

"Please!" Midge said. "I'm trying to think! I do remember something that might help. . . . Wait. One morning I saw Vic come out of a house in the Village . . . He was carrying skis and a bag. He got into a car that was waiting for him . . . There was a girl in the car, they drove off. . . ."

"Skis and a bag," Larry said. "A suitcase? Then he probably lived in that house."

"Yes. I remember thinking, so that's where Vic Jacoby lives."

"Now," Larry said, "we're getting someplace. Where was the house?"

"Yes, where was the house?" Midge said. "Where could it have been, that house?"

Larry groaned. "Oh, no!"

"Now don't get mad at me! I go all to pieces when people get mad at me!"

"Sit down, Midge," Larry said.

"Thank you," Midge said, and sat down.

"One morning," Larry said, "you were walking along a street in the Village . . . Try to remember where you were going."

"I was going to see a girl from Bennington. She was having a Sunday brunch."

"And where did your friend live, Midge?"

"Bleecker Street."

"Was the house you saw Vic come out of on Bleecker?"

"No. No, wait. . . . I had stopped at Sutter's bakery and bought some croissants to take for brunch, and I crossed Greenwich Avenue at the ladies' jail there and I kept going straight . . . and I saw Vic and his skis . . . Let's see, Sutter's is on West Tenth Street. . . . I was still on West

Tenth when I saw Vic . . . the house was halfway down the block from Greenwich Avenue on the uptown side of the street. You know, I think I would recognize it if I saw it again. If it's still there, if it hasn't been remodeled or something. . . ."

"Let's go see," Larry said.

She had telephoned the theater and told the stage manager that she was going out, but would keep in constant touch with him. She had shoved her feet into teetering, definitely un-hippy high-heeled shoes and slipped into a suede coat, and they were ready to go. They did not see an empty cab until they had walked to Second Avenue. Before Larry could make a move to hail it, Midge had put both her little fingers in her mouth and whistled a blast that rocked him back on his heels. The cab skittered to a stop before them like a startled fawn. As they climbed into it, the driver said to Larry, "Man, that is the greatest, the most whistle I ever heard."

"It wasn't me," Larry said, feeling unheroic.

"It was you, miss?" the driver said incredulously. "Where did you learn that?"

"My mother taught me," Midge said. "The ladies' jail, please. Tenth Street between Sixth and Greenwich."

"You got friends in there?" the driver said, grinning. "You going to blow down the walls like that deal in the Good Book and free your friends the ladies?"

"None of my friends are ladies," Midge said.

Twenty minutes later they were standing in the middle of the Tenth Street block off Greenwich Avenue. Midge decided that the house they were looking for was the one with a battered clump of shedding privet hedge in its areaway. They consulted the posting in the vestibule; there was no V.

Jacoby listed. The janitor, they discovered, lived next door. He answered their ringing of his bell with a can of beer in his hand. He was in good humor, inclined to be cooperative, even friendly, a man whose day's work was done, and well done.

Larry tilted his head to the right. "You're the janitor for the house next door?"

"The superintendent," Midge said. "He's the superintendent."

"The pay is the same either way, miss, but yeah, I have next door."

"Do you remember a tenant named Jacoby?" Larry asked. "We know he was there about three years ago. We don't know how long before, or how long after."

"I don't know him," the superintendent said. "But I only been working here little over a year."

"Oh," Larry said.

"Damn," Midge said. "Do you know where the old super is?"

"No. All I know is he's dead."

"Oh, I'm sorry," Midge said, and she meant it.

"Could you tell us," Larry said, "which tenants have been there longer than three years?"

"Well, I guess Kohler's been there longer than anyone else. Or maybe Jensen, but she's never home nights. Kohler is your best bet now."

"Is that Mr. Kohler?" Larry asked.

"Yeah. Don't tell him I sent you. It's kinda late and he's a sourpuss."

They rang the Kohler bell and when they reached the top of the second flight of stairs, they found Mr. Kohler waiting for them in the doorway of his apartment. They saw immediately what the superintendent had meant. Kohler was a sourpuss; the scowl lines on his face were etched deep, although he was still in his early thirties. He was of medium height and rather scrawny. His scalp beneath his sparse, sandy-colored hair was an angry red, as though he had just given himself a violent and hopeful treatment up there.

"Mr. Kohler?" Larry asked.

He wasn't ready to admit that. "Who are you? What do you want?"

"My name is Larry Towers."

"So?" He regarded Larry's beard with distaste and the hair on Larry's head with envy.

"And this is Miss Redding."

"So?" His eyes insolently cased her figure; his scowl diminished.

"Hello, Mr. Kohler," Midge said in her special way.

Mr. Kohler's leer was even less attractive than his scowl. "Something you want?" Then his attitude turned suspicious. "You got a petition for me to sign? I don't sign any petitions, no matter for what."

Larry was about to answer him, then thought better of it. Midge was the one who should take care of this, and she did.

"No petition, Mr. Kohler," she said brightly. "You were here when Vic Jacoby lived in this building, weren't you?"

The scowl was back on his face, deeper, blacker than before. "Jacoby. Yes, he had the apartment right above."

Midge laughed. "Did he make a lot of noise?"

"Why do you say that?"

"Well, you aren't all smiles, hearing his name. Didn't you like him?"

"I hardly knew him. He thought he was too good for

anyone around here. High-hat, a big shot. Why you coming to me about him?"

"We're trying to find him."

"How would I know where he is?" Kohler said. "I couldn't care less."

"Well, maybe you can tell us something," Midge said, "that will give us a lead."

"And maybe," Kohler said, "I wouldn't tell you if I could. Jacoby never did me any favors."

Midge looked to Larry for help.

"We want to find him," Larry said, "to warn him that his life is in danger. Someone is trying to kill him."

"Someone is trying to kill Jacoby?" Kohler said slowly. Then a sudden fever of excitement flushed his face. "How do you know that? Come in. Come in and tell me about it. Somebody's trying to kill Jacoby!"

He ushered them into his living room, pointed out places for them to sit. He switched off the television set, sat on the edge of a chair. As Larry talked, he kept interrupting, asking questions, wanting to know details. A look of morbid satisfaction was taking over his face.

"There was this one woman, Mrs. Grant," he said. "And there were two men, at least two men in the car?"

Larry nodded.

Kohler's breath exploded in a long whistle. "A gang operation! It looks like a gang operation! The rackets, that's what it looks like. The Mafia!"

"The Mafia!" Midge said, her breath exploding, too. "Vic Jacoby and the Mafia? You're crazy!"

"Wait, now you just wait a minute!" Kohler was unable to sit still any longer; he bounced to his feet. "Now this explains a whole lot about Jacoby. I always thought there was something fishy about him. I always wondered where he got the money for an apartment like mine and those slick clothes of his. And all those trips off to Europe he took, with that fancy airplane luggage of his. I asked around about him. People in the building said he didn't go to work at any regular time in the morning, like I go to the office, or come home at any regular time at night. I had to ask around, I couldn't get anything at all out of him. He wouldn't even pass the time of day with anyone here. . . . Good morning or good evening, that's the most I ever got out of him, if that. What I mean is, he didn't have any visible means of support!" His voice rose in triumph. "You understand? Glamour-boy Jacoby, he didn't have any *visible means of support!*"

Larry looked at Midge. She was regarding Kohler with pure loathing. Her eyes met Larry's and he shook his head at her. She got the signal; she sank back on the sofa, indicating that she was out of it. She was not going to try to defend Vic Jacoby against this weirdo.

"He could have been a rich boy," Larry said. "He could have had money of his own, an inheritance."

"Yeah, he was that type. Money of his own. An inheritance. Important family, all that. The élite. Except for what happened the last night he was here. That doesn't fit."

"What happened?" Larry said.

"It was about a year and a half ago. I was coming home from the office and up ahead of me on Tenth Street I saw Mr. Jacoby. In between us was a Sicilian type . . ."

"What's a Sicilian type?" Midge said.

"Gangster-looking," Kohler said. "Of course, I didn't see that until later. After Jacoby came in here and this type went across the street and stationed himself there. Then I could see he was a gangster type. Sicilian."

"Stationed himself?" Midge asked.

"To watch the house," Kohler said, his eyes glowing. "I saw him from up here. He was looking up at Jacoby's apartment. About an hour later another goon joined him. . . ."

Midge lost her composure. "What's a goon? How do you know a goon when you see one?"

Kohler looked at Midge and smiled knowingly. "You were one of his, weren't you?"

"One of his what?"

"Dames."

Midge moved up out of the sofa. Her fists were clenched for combat. Larry stepped in quickly. "All right," he said, "the second man looked like another goon to you."

"He had Mafia written all over him," Kohler said. "The two of them talked it over for a minute or two, then they came across the street and into the house. I don't know how they got in the street door. Maybe they busted it open like they did Jacoby's door. I heard them go past here, up the stairs. I went out into the hall. They knocked on his door, then they smashed it open. They were in Jacoby's place for like half an hour, then they went away."

"You didn't call the police, good citizen," Midge said, "during that half hour, good citizen?"

"I didn't want to get mixed up in anything. Was it my business?"

"They could have been killing Vic!" Midge said.

"No, he was chicken." Kohler laughed and justified his laugh saying, "Jacoby had flown the coop. He was gone. I guess he knew he was on the spot. He must have seen those two goons from his window and got away across the roof, I guess, because I never saw him again."

Larry said, "What were the goons doing in his apartment

for half an hour?"

"Searching the place," Kohler said. "After they were gone, I went up. The place had been ransacked. They were looking for something, all right. My guess is money. I think he was holding out on them for his take from dope or prostitution or something."

"Vic?" Midge said. "Vic Jacoby?"

"I said I always knew there was something fishy about him," Kohler said. "He doublecrossed the Mafia. He's on their rub-out list. That's who's trying to kill him."

"And you like that!" Midge said, clenching her fists again.

Larry prevented Kohler from answering; he knew that would result in Midge's beating him to a pulp. He said, "You don't admire Jacoby, but I'm sure you don't wish him anything more than bad luck. You don't want him dead."

The thought of the infinite put a charitable look on Kohler's face. "No, I don't especially want anyone dead."

"Good boy," Midge said. "We, the living, thank you."

"Don't be sarcastic at me," Kohler said. "It isn't my fault they chased your boy friend away. How did a girl that looks like you get mixed up with an oily wop creep like Jacoby?"

Midge took a deep breath.

"Don't bother," Larry said.

"Aren't we wasting our time here?" Midge said. "To say the least?"

"But let's keep trying." Larry turned back to Kohler. "You said that Jacoby wasn't friendly with anyone in the building?"

"Not that I know of."

"But people came to see him, didn't they?"

"Sure, lots of people. But I don't know any of them. He never introduced me. But, well, there's Theresa. Maybe she knows something about him."

"Who's Theresa?"

"She cleans for me three mornings a week. She used to work for Jacoby, too."

"Maybe we could talk to her."

"I've got her phone number," Kohler said. "I'll call her and see."

Theresa was not at home, but her sister said that she was sitting with some children while their parents were at the theater. The sister told Kohler the name and address of the parents; he looked the number up in the book. He talked to Theresa; she would be only too glad to help his friends if she could. They should come right over.

"Thank you," Larry said.

"I did it for Miss Redding," Kohler said. "I want her to find out what a bad deal this Jacoby is and forget about him."

"Thank you, dream boy," Midge said. "Thanks for everything."

They walked to Sixth Avenue, looking for a taxi all the way, of course, not finding one. Midge was in a fever of impatience to talk to Theresa about her former employer.

"It's all right, Midge," Larry said. "She'll be there for a while. The parents are at the theater and . . ."

Midge clapped her hand over her mouth. "The theater! Oh, good Lord, I've got to call the stage manager! Oh, good Lord, where's there a telephone?"

There was a drugstore on the opposite corner and Midge jay-raced across the street and into it.

"It's okay," she reported a minute later. "The curtain's up on the third act and Tony is still in good health. It looks like she'll survive. Charley says I can take the rest of the night off."

CHAPTER 5

"I DON'T BELIEVE it!" Theresa said. "I don't believe a word of it! Why would anyone want to kill a nice young man like Mr. Jacoby?"

"Mr. Kohler doesn't think Mr. Jacoby is a nice young man," Midge said.

She told Theresa what Kohler thought of Vic Jacoby. Theresa's pleasant, wrinkled face darkened with each word; her eyes behind thick, steel-rimmed glasses sparkled, her iron-gray hair bristled, her shoulders tensed with indignation. Her outcry, Larry feared, would rouse the children she was being paid to keep in bed and sound asleep.

"I don't believe a word of it!" she said again. "That Mr. Kohler, I never did like him, little as I ever see of him. I'll never work for him again. I quit! Here and now!"

"But those two . . . the goons Kohler said he saw. What do you think about that?" Larry asked. "I don't think Kohler made them up. I don't think he has enough imagination."

"I don't know what to think about that," Theresa said.

"All I know is that Mr. Jacoby didn't run away because any goon fellows was after him. He was going away. He told me so. He told me one morning he was going on a trip. It would probably be a long trip. He was going to leave that night. He had given up the apartment, he said. . . . That's a furnished place he rented. None of his things was there except his clothes . . . and he gave me two weeks' pay. He said when he came back and got another place he'd call me."

"But he didn't call you?"

"No, that's true."

"So," Larry said, "it could be that he was planning to leave because he was in some trouble, and the goons just speeded up his take-off a little."

"Hey!" Midge said. "Excuse me, but whose side are you on?"

"My side," Larry said. "The life I'm trying to save may still be my own. Theresa, that last time you saw him, did Mr. Jacoby tell you where he was going?"

The woman didn't answer. She was staring hard at Larry, her face puzzled. "Don't I know you from somewheres, Mr. Towers? You seem awful familiar to me."

"No, I don't think so," Larry said. "Do you remember, Theresa? Did he say where he was going?"

"Europe. He didn't say where exactly. But he was always flying off someplace over there, Europe or someplace."

"He did it regularly? As though it was business?"

Theresa looked at him in surprise. "Well, sure it was business. That's the reason Mr. Jacoby traveled so much. He was an importer. He imported things from abroad. Olives."

"Olives?" Larry said.

"Olives!" Midge said.

Theresa nodded. "Oh, yes, that's what his business was. If

it wasn't for him, there wouldn't be enough olives in America."

Larry looked at Midge. "Do you think that's right? That Vic Jacoby was an importer of olives?"

"Well," Midge said, "I never saw him with a jar, but why couldn't he import olives? Somebody has to."

Larry nodded. "So Vic is in olives. Dangerous game, olives."

"You don't believe Theresa, do you? You can't think that Vic was in some honest, perfectly legitimate business like olives. You'd rather believe Kohler."

Larry shrugged, turned to Theresa. "Did Mr. Jacoby have an office?"

She seemed surprised at the question. "Why, yes, sure. All businessmen have offices."

"Do you know where it was?"

"No. He never said."

"Did you know the phone number?"

"No. Why would I know the phone number?"

"In case anyone called while you were there. You could give them his office number."

"Well, he never gave me his office number. If somebody called, I just took the message. Look, Mr. Towers . . ."

"Yes?"

"I swear to goodness I've seen you before tonight. Don't you remember seeing me from somewhere?"

He shook his head. "I'm afraid not," he said. "These messages you took, Theresa. Do you remember any of them?"

"Oh, no, it's been a long time ago, over a year. Well, but wait. There was one lady who used to call a lot just before Mr. Jacoby left. Her name was Miss Tyler. She would say, Ask Mr. Jacoby to call Miss Tyler."

Larry sighed a discouraged sigh. "There must be hundreds of Miss Tylers in Greater New York. She always said just Miss Tyler? Never Miss Mary or Lucy or Jane Tyler?"

"Always just Miss Tyler. But wait a minute. Once I was there when he called her back, and I did hear him say her name. It was an unusual name, a name I never heard before, so maybe I can remember it. It was almost like the big city in Italy. Rome. He called her Roma, with an *a* instead of an *e*. Roma."

"Roma Tyler," Larry said. "Midge, does that mean anything to you? Did you ever know a Roma Tyler?"

"No," Midge said, "but I think I should get to know her. I think we both should, and as soon as possible."

When the pert and pretty little maid, in a chic black and white uniform, who had opened the door on the twelfth floor of the fashionably old Fifth Avenue apartment house, came back to the hall where they were waiting, she had been told what to do about them. As she led them down a corridor to a small, pine-paneled study, Larry could hear the discreet buzz of quiet chatter, soft and modulated laughter, the clink of glass and ice and silver, the nonintruding music of a hi-fi.

They were kept waiting, as though in punishment for their intrusion, a good ten minutes. And when Miss Roma Tyler finally did make an appearance, the look on her lovely and patrician face showed that she would have preferred to keep them waiting even longer. He should have known, Larry thought, from the prettiness of the maid that the mistress would be no dog, but he had not expected this. Her voice when he had telephoned was waspish and unfriendly and had left him unprepared for this vision before them.

She stood regarding them from the doorway, tall and slim in an ice-blue dress glittering with thousands of ice-blue beads. Her hair was blue-black, her eyes still another shade of blue, her skin cream-colored, her features perfect. Larry glanced at Midge and saw what he might have expected to see—she was staring at Vic Jacoby's beautiful friend with a mixture of awe and dismay.

Roma Tyler did not bother to greet them. "Really," she said, her voice as cold and hostile as it had been on the phone, "this is very annoying, very inconsiderate of you to insist upon seeing me tonight. As I told you, I am entertaining some friends."

"Miss Tyler," Larry said, "when I said it was a matter of life and death, I meant it. That was not a figure of speech."

A smile began to curve her lips, then disappeared abruptly. She said, "You're serious? You mean that Vic is literally in danger?"

"Yes."

"Someone is actually trying to murder him?"

"More than one person is trying to kill him," Larry said. "There seems to be some sort of organized group effort to get Vic Jacoby. They've tried; so far they've missed. . . ."

The sharp intake of her breath stopped him. The blue eyes had darkened, turned almost black in anger. A flush started at her neckline, spread furiously up her cheeks. She stared at him and tried to speak. No sound came out.

"What is it?" Larry asked.

It was a moment before she found her voice. "What is it?" she repeated. "Yes. That's what I was about to ask you. What kind of a trick is this? What kind of a nasty practical joke are you trying to play?"

Midge said, "Miss Tyler, listen to me . . ."

Roma Tyler swung to face her. "I don't know what he's told you, what he's made you believe. I don't care who he says he is. He's Vic Jacoby."

"No," Midge said, "that's what it's all about. Everyone thinks he's Vic, and that's the whole trouble. . . ."

"No, my dear, believe me, he is Vic Jacoby," Roma said, and smiled. Her anger and her shocked surprise were under control now; she was incensed that anyone should try to play such an outrageous prank on her, but she was patient. She turned to Larry. "Really, Vic, how could you do this to me? And, in God's name, why?"

"There you have it," Larry said. "That's it. Why, in God's name, would Vic Jacoby do this to you? Or is he the type who would grow a beard and get himself up in clothes like these in order to play, as you said, a nasty, practical joke?"

"Miss Tyler," Midge said, "I knew Vic Jacoby. You did, too. You must know he wouldn't do a thing like this to you, not to anybody."

There was a pause and then Roma Tyler said slowly, "I think you're right. Yes, you have me there. I don't believe that Vic is capable of such a thing. Then someone actually is trying to kill him. It's true . . . No, it can't be true."

"Yes," Larry said, "it's true. Let me fill you in. My name is Larry Towers. Until three weeks ago I had never heard the name Vic Jacoby. I had never been in New York before in my life. I have never seen you before tonight. I don't blame you for finding it difficult to believe me. There is a gang of would-be murderers around who absolutely refuse to believe me. They are out to kill Vic Jacoby and they think that I'm their man."

"And so you, of course," Roma said, "are trying to look as

little like Vic as possible."

"That's right."

"Who is trying to kill Vic?" she asked. "How?"

When he had finished telling her, she was still staring at him, intently studying his face. She shook her head. "It's incredible. Yes, I can see how difficult it would be for you to convince anyone you were not Vic Jacoby. Your features, your profile . . . they're Vic's."

"I would gladly give them back to him," Larry said.

"I'm sure you would. And I understand why you are so anxious to find him. Unfortunately, I can't help you."

"You don't know where he is?"

"No. I never really knew Vic very well and I haven't seen him for . . . oh, it's been well over a year. He went away. I haven't heard from him. Or of him, either. He . . . well, he neglected to keep in touch."

She smiled, but it was a rueful smile. It was a humiliating thing, Larry realized, for this girl, this perfect, golden girl, to admit that there was a living, or perhaps even deceased male who had neglected to keep in touch.

He glanced at Midge. For her to hear that Vic Jacoby had dropped out of the life of this glorious girl was a pleasant surprise. Her face lightened. But then it fell as she realized that this was not good news. Roma Tyler could not help them.

CHAPTER 6

"WHEN EXACTLY," Larry asked, "was the last time you saw Vic?"

"Just before he went abroad," Roma said. "That was a year ago last spring. I don't remember dates."

"He told you he was going? He planned the trip?"

"Yes, of course. Well, not exactly. It was a very sudden trip, unexpected. He called me one afternoon to say he was leaving that night. But he did call me. Why?"

"There's a man in Jacoby's old apartment house who says that this trip was inspired by a couple of goons who followed Vic and broke into his apartment and searched it."

Her eyes widened. "Vic and goons?" she asked incredulously. "Vic Jacoby and a couple of goons? That's nonsense."

"The neighbor's idea is that he was mixed up with some gangster mob. The Mafia even."

"The whole idea is preposterous," Roma said. "I didn't know much about Vic, he was kind of a mystery-type guy, but gangsters, mobsters . . . no, never."

"Would you believe olives?" Larry asked.

"Olives?"

"His cleaning woman says he was in olives. That was the reason for his trips abroad, to import olives. They were routine, regular business trips."

"Business trips?" Roma said, and laughed aloud. "Oh, no! Nobody in the world would be less likely to take a business trip than Vic. Wherever he went he went for pleasure."

"What did he use for money?"

Roma shrugged. "One has money," she said, "or one hasn't any money. Vic seemed to have it."

"Inherited money?"

"I suppose so."

"So," Larry said, "you don't think Vic was in olives."

"Not in olives, not in anything."

"Not in the rackets, not in the Mafia."

"No, never. Vic could not be so stupid. He enjoyed life too much to risk it like that. He was a worldwide playboy, that's what Vic was. A jet-set leader."

"But," Larry said, "certain people are trying to kill him. Why? Not because he's a worldwide playboy. Or a jet-set leader. That can't be the reason."

"No," Roma said slowly. "I see what you mean."

"Look," Larry said, "let's start with the money. You know Vic Jacoby had some money, enough to live pretty well, but you're not sure it was inherited."

"No. Actually, no. I took that for granted."

"Because he didn't seem to you to have any visible means of support. Now just for the hell of it, let's say that Vic, honestly or dishonestly, did earn a living. How do you think he might have done it, First, remember that he traveled a good deal. . . ."

"Yes," Roma said. "And maybe all those trips weren't for pleasure. The pattern seems wrong to me now. Sometimes he would stay only a few days in New York, then be off somewhere, for any length of time. Almost as though . . ." She stopped, puzzled.

"As though," Larry said, "he might possibly have been taking orders from someone?"

"That's what I was thinking, yes. And I was thinking about his secrecy about himself. Apparently he never told anyone anything—just let them speculate. His neighbor thought he was a gangster, his maid thought he was an importer, I thought he was a playboy. He let us all think whatever we wanted."

"Then," Larry said, "if the neighbor's story about the goons is true, and I think it is . . ."

Roma nodded. "That adds danger. Vic could have been doing something dangerous."

"And now there are people, an organized group of people, trying to murder him. And," Larry said, "that I know to be true."

There was a moment's silence, then Roma said softly, "Yes, it could be. It's almost impossible to believe, and yet it could be. I've never dreamed I knew anybody in espionage."

"Espionage!" Midge squeaked. "Vic Jacoby a spy!"

"Let's say an agent, Miss Redding," Roma said, and smiled. "An agent, a valuable member of the C.I.A."

"Secret Agent Jacoby," Midge said. "Oh, no!"

"Can you think of anything," Larry asked Roma, "that would contradict that?"

"No," Roma said slowly, thinking it out, "no, I can't. In fact, it would explain a great deal to me about Vic. So," she said bluntly, "Vic is very possibly involved in espionage.

That is why his life is in danger. They want to kill him, but they're trying to kill you by mistake. What are you going to do about it?"

"There's a policeman," Larry said, "a Detective Lieutenant Corso. He's doing what he can for me. Maybe if this makes sense, he'll be able to do more. Like get in touch with the C.I.A."

"I hope so." Her smile at Larry was a warmer one than he had thought her capable of. "I don't want anything to happen to either of you. And if you find out anything about Vic, will you let me know?"

"Will you mind," Larry said, "if I call you while you're having a party?"

"I'm sorry about that," Roma said. She included Midge in her apology. "I'm sorry I was rude. It never occurred to me that it could actually be a matter of life and death. I thought, of course . . . Oh, dear Lord, it's just really hitting me now! Someone is actually trying to murder Vic Jacoby!"

"Well, at the moment," Larry said, "they're looking for me, you know. So you don't have to worry about Vic. Not at the moment."

They stood at the corner for five minutes without seeing an empty cab. Fifth Avenue was deserted of buses as far north as they could see. Larry decided that the quickest way to get downtown to Detective Lieutenant Corso's precinct would be the Lexington Avenue subway. He suggested he take Midge to her apartment first; she insisted that she go with him. Maybe she could help, she said. Detective Corso might want to ask her some questions about Vic Jacoby.

They walked east to Madison and then turned north and started uptown toward Ninety-sixth Street. The had taken only a few steps when Larry touched Midge's elbow. "Don't look back," he said softly. "Keep on going. . . ."

"What's wrong?"

"When we came out of Roma Tyler's building, there was a man standing across the street. I think he may be following us."

"How do we find out?"

"Open your purse, drop it, make sure it spills."

"Now?"

"I'll tell you." In a moment he said, "Now."

The purse fell from Midge's hand, hit the sidewalk and its contents spewed out in a widening circle. "Damn!" Midge said in a loud and exasperated voice.

They crouched together to retrieve the scattered objects that had spilled from her bag. "Not too quickly," Larry whispered. "Let's take our time." He listened for footsteps. He heard heels click on the sidewalk, three times, four, and then they stopped. He looked covertly behind him; a man stood before the window of a shop. In the glow of the night light he could see that the man was tall; he wore a sweater, tight black levis, their bottoms stuffed into ski boots.

"Have we got everything?" Larry asked, his voice at normal pitch.

"I think so," Midge said, playing it with him. "Everything that matters. Maybe I've lost two or three cents, but I can afford it."

They walked on up Madison, his hand on her arm. When they reached the next street, Ninety-fifth, he held her still for a moment. He heard the click of boot heels behind them come to a stop. His hand tightened on her arm and they walked on.

"We are definitely being followed," Midge said.

"Yes," Larry said, "we are definitely being followed. To be more accurate, you and Vic Jacoby are being followed."

"This is the first time," Midge said, "that this has ever happened to Vic and me. Honest."

"I wish I could believe you," Larry said.

"If we could find a cab," Midge said, "and ski boots couldn't find one, that would be nice."

"You can never find a cab when you need one," Larry said. "You're old enough to know that."

"Sometimes I find one," Midge said.

"Do it now," Larry said.

"Don't pin me down," Midge said. "It only happened once or twice. Once mostly."

They walked east across Ninety-sixth Street, across Park Avenue, down the slope to Lexington Avenue. The ski boots heels clicked behind them. They passed a branch city library.

"That reminds me," Midge said. "I have a book overdue."

"Much overdue?" Larry said. "I mean is it seriously overdue?"

"You're being nice to me," Midge said, "and I appreciate it. I'm a little hysterical. This is the first time in my life I've ever been scared, really scared. Are you scared?"

"Hold my hand," Larry said.

She did. She said, "Your hand isn't shaking."

"But I'm scared," Larry said. "Of course I'm beginning to get used to it."

"That creep!" Midge said. "Wearing ski boots! I bet he's never been on skis in his life."

"You sound as if you don't like him," Larry said. "He's only doing his job."

"Sorry," Midge said.

"Somebody has to do it," Larry said. "Follow Vic Jacoby,

knock him off."

"You sound bitter."

"No," Larry said. "I'm glad to do it for Vic."

"That's hysterical dialogue," Midge said. "Yes, you're scared and I like you for it. We have something in common."

"Let's not hold onto it," Larry said.

"Here's the subway," Midge said. "Are we still going to take the subway?"

He nodded and, pulling Midge after him, he darted down the steps into the subway station. They walked quickly past the change booth, not stopping to exchange money for tokens. They hurried up five steps of the opposite entrance, the one across the street. On the fifth step he stopped, stooped down and looked across to the stairs they had just descended. In a moment he saw a pair of ski boots step into sight. The ski boots, then the tight black levis.

He rose and jerked Midge up the rest of the stairs, congratulating himself on his maneuver. Ski Boots would take for granted that they had gone through the turnstiles and out onto the platform to wait for the next train. By now he would be putting his token into the slot and moving onto the platform, looking for them. They had successfully shaken Ski Boots. All they had to do now was get away from this place.

They stepped out onto the sidewalk and, across the street, he saw the car. Of course there were many cars like that, with two men sitting in the front seat. But he had a memory-image of the same car with the same two men in it moving past him on a country road and shooting bullets at him.

Tightening his grip on Midge's arm, he crossed the street. From the far corner he saw the car move down Lexington Avenue after them. It could still mean nothing; it could still be the coincidence of a similar car with two men in it, one of them did not necessarily have to be holding a gun he meant to use on him. But he had to know. He swung around the corner into Ninety-fifth Street, a one-way street, westbound. The car followed them into it, heading east. Now, too late, he knew for certain, and he saw the trap he and Midge had made for themselves.

On both sides of the street were black, silent buildings, all marked for demolition, or high wooden fences where the houses had already been razed. The cars that lined both curbs were dark and empty, the sidewalks deserted. The car crawled along behind them, the glare of its headlights reaching for them.

He turned at one of the blacked-out houses, pulled Midge up the two shallow steps to the stoop. The door into the vestibule had been removed. They flattened themselves against the wall. The headlights brightened the street outside, and then passed by. Now, if they could get back to Lexington before the men in the car realized they were behind them, they had a chance. He looked up the block toward Lexington and saw Ski Boots start down the street. He looked the other way and saw the car stop, double-park down near the corner of Third Avenue. A man got out, started walking back, back toward Ski Boots.

"We're surrounded," Larry said.

Midge made a frightened sound.

Larry turned back into the vestibule and threw all his weight against the inside door. It trembled in its frame without giving, but its lower panel gave way. Larry dropped to his knees and found the opening.

"Get inside," he said to Midge. "Quick."

She snaked through the hole and he followed her. He

heard sounds outside. Ski Boots and the man in the car had met almost in front of them. He could hear their voices.

Carefully, hardly daring to breathe, he lifted the panel of the door and fitted it back in its frame. He whispered in Midge's ear.

"Let's get away from here."

"Let's," she whispered back.

Hand in hand they groped through the total blackness of the hallway. At the end of it they found a door which, Larry guessed rightly, would lead down into the basement. They made their way down the steps and to the back of the house. A door there opened onto what had once been a back yard. Now what they saw in the dim reflection of the big city night light was chaos and destruction everywhere. Piles of rubbish, brick and stone, wood and plaster filled the entire block. Between the piles great black holes yawned. The ugly old block was being completely demolished for a hopeful new one.

Stumbling and slipping, they got through the jungle of debris and to the nearest of the few still standing buildings on the opposite side of the block, the Ninety-fourth Street side. They found an empty door frame and went through it. Through the window boardings some street light filtered into the room they stood in, a beacon to safety. They started toward it.

The floor beneath them gave way. There was a grinding roar as it collapsed, and they were falling down with the collapsing building, down into darkness and dust and chaos.

Then there was a sudden, echoing silence.

"Midge!" he said. "Midge, where are you?"

She did not answer.

CHAPTER 7

THE THREE CHILDREN sat on the stoop of the five-story building that had twenty small apartments in it. Two of the children were boys approximately the same age, seven. The girl was the sister of one of them, smaller, tiny really, a year and a half younger. She was looking anxiously at her brother, waiting for him to speak. He was staring across the street at the row of old, low-rent houses, trying to think of the correct answer to the question his friend had asked him.

"Hey, Mike," his friend said, "you fall asleep or something?"

He grinned; he liked his friend to call him Mike. Then his face clouded. "I dunno," he said. "How'd I know, Bud?"

"Can't you make a guess?" Bud asked.

"Until she gets big enough to take care of herself, I guess."

"Hey, Izzy," Bud said, "when you gonna get big enough to take care of yourself?"

"I don't wanna take care of myself," Izzy said. "I want to play with you and Mike."

"All your life?"

"How long's that?" Izzy asked.

"Oh, let her alone, Bud," Mike said. "She don't know nothing."

The door inside the vestibule began to open. Bud jumped down off the stoop, ran into the areaway beside it to hide. An old woman came out of the house.

"Hello, Mrs. Jones," Izzy said. "Good morning."

The woman ignored her.

When the old lady had crept down to the sidewalk and her back was to the stoop, Mike whistled the all-clear signal to Bud.

Bud came back, sat on the bottom step. "What'll we do?" he asked.

"It's Sunday," Mike said. "The men ain't working."

"Yeah," Bud said, "but it isn't much fun with Izzy."

"I'll take care of her," Mike said. "You don't have to. C'mon, let's go!"

They walked, skipped and ran up the block to Third Avenue, crossed it and went on into the next block at Ninety-fifth Street. They sat on the fourth stoop from the corner. The building behind it had been abandoned; it was marked by the tape on its few remaining unsmashed upper story windows for demolition. The lower-story windows were still boarded up.

When the children were sure that no one was looking, they darted into the vestibule which stood without any outside door. Bud pushed open a loose panel in the bottom of the inside door. He crawled through the opening, then Izzy slithered through it, then Mike. Bud carefully put the panel back in place, made sure it would stay there.

He led the way down the dilapidated stairway into the basement, then out into the back of the building. The far end of the block had been completely leveled and had already been enclosed by a tall plywood fence. A crane stood near the center of the block, the iron ball dangling from its chain beside the brick wall that was next in line for attack. The children, with Mike helping Izzy, picked their way through and over the debris. Suddenly Bud grabbed the other two and pulled them down behind a pile of splintered lumber.

"I saw a man," he whispered.

"What's he doing here?" Mike whispered in protest. "It's Sunday."

Bud held his finger to his lips. In a minute he dared stand up and peek over the stack of lumber. He saw the man moving away toward the row of houses that were already gutted of plumbing, windows and floors, awaiting the final destruction of the iron ball. The man moved out of sight behind a huge bulldozer.

"He's gone," Bud said. "But we got to be real quiet."

"Real quiet," Mike said. "You understand, Izzy?"

"Like this?" she said, whispering.

"What?" Mike said.

She held her finger to her lips.

Midge's hand tightened on Larry's arm. He nodded; he, too, had heard the footsteps above them. There seemed to be more than one person, and the footsteps were light, as though they were being made on tiptoe, as though whoever was moving above them was being cautious, stealthy. The alarm in Midge's eyes told him that she was thinking as he was; they didn't dare to make a move or to cry out for help. The people just a floor above them could be the ones from whom they escaped in the night, still hunting for them. Then the steps faded away, but Midge's hand did not relax on his arm.

The night had been a long horror. Larry had been thrown clear of the cave-in. He had called out to Midge and she had not answered. He had used up a few matches he had without finding her. Then, frantically, he had groped about in total blackness, crawling on his hands and knees, clawing blindly at the brick and mortar and lumber, afraid that she had been buried beneath the debris. At last he had heard a faint moan and he made his way to her. She had been knocked unconscious by the fall, but except for a swollen bruise on one temple, she was unhurt.

Waiting out the night in the cold black silence had been painful and gruesome. From time to time they had reminded each other in encouraging whispers that they were alive; they refrained from thinking about how long that condition might last, how long it would be before the men who were following them would find their accidental refuge.

Daylight had finally done its best to come down to them; it was, at best, a dark shade of dismal gray. Up under the ceiling of the cellar Larry saw a small window, no more than three feet by three, and it was barred. He went to stand below it and discovered why more light did not come through to them. A sheet of metal, stacked against the back of their house, obstructed the window and created a lean-to. The right side of the piled sheets was blocked by the rubble, but at the base of the left side there was a hole about the size of a bushel basket. That was their only source of light. It was meager, and Larry was only barely able to see what sort of hole they had got themselves into, and the circumstances of their precipitous arrival there.

The floor above them, he could see now, had collapsed only to about the center of the building. Fortunately, to put it mildly, Midge and he had been sent sprawling toward the rear of the house where the floor above them was still holding. The interior walls of the place had come crashing down, filling the hole through which they had fallen with bricks and mortar, lumber and debris. Their living quarters, their breathing space was an ample thirty feet by approximately twenty. They weren't crowded; they could not, Larry thought, complain to the landlord about that.

He moved to the foot of the miniature, indoor avalanche. It completely plugged the hole in the ceiling. His first thought was, of course, to find a way out of their prison. Experimentally he tugged at a piece of lumber. When that maneuver created the sound of further falling rubble, he had a second thought. He knew that he must make no noise that might attract the attention of the enemy who were certainly still lurking about, still searching for them. This enemy would not give up and go home; they were dedicated to the demise of Vic Jacoby. He decided not to burden Midge with this unpleasant but realistic surmise, but she had read his thoughts.

"We can't even try to get out, can we?" she whispered. "They're out there, maybe right out there right now. They can hear any noise we make."

"Well," he said, "let's not be overpessimistic."

"Don't baby me, Larry. They must have kept watch in the streets all night. They know we're still in here. And they'll be in here looking for us."

"I'm afraid so, Midge."

"They're not stupid."

"No, let's not underestimate the enemy."

"So," she said, reasoning just as he had reasoned, "we can't risk making any noise even trying to get out."

"I'm afraid you're right again, Midge."

"Actually, it doesn't look to me as though we could get

out no matter how much noise we make. You're afraid I'm right again, aren't you?"

"Afraid so."

"So, to put it bluntly, there is no escape."

"Not at the moment."

"Not at the moment," Midge said, "but after that? Oh, of course! The workmen. The workmen should be coming any minute now, shouldn't they? They'll get us out, they'll call the police . . ."

"Midge, I have bad news for you. It won't happen that soon. Today is Sunday."

She groaned. "Yes, today is Sunday. They won't be coming until tomorrow. Well," she said, and managed a grin, "it could be worse. Tomorrow could be Labor Day. But bright and early tomorrow morning the workmen will be here and they'll get us out, unless . . ."

"Don't say it, Midge."

"I won't. I was going to say unless the gunmen find us first, but I won't. But it's kind of depressing, isn't it? They do have all of twenty-four hours to find us."

"Yes, but maybe we're hard to find."

"As hard to find as a needle in a haystack," Midge said, "if we keep as quiet as mice. Larry!"

"Yes?"

"I have hope!"

"Your hope is justified, guaranteed. Ten years from now we'll look back on this . . . and Vic Jacoby will laugh."

There was enough light then, just enough, for Larry to read the time his watch was telling; it was eight o'clock. He watched the hands drag around as though they were tired of it all, completely exhausted.

It was a few minutes after ten that they heard the footsteps overhead come and go and they froze. But for a while afterward there was silence above. All they could hear was the occasional muted roar of a nearby bus or truck. Then, suddenly, there was a rustle of sound close to them, and the shaft of light coming through the small window lessened to almost a blackout. Midge's hand found Larry's again, clung to it. They moved together to a corner, out of sight of the window, and huddled in it.

In a minute there was another sound. "Me first," a little girl's voice said. "It's my cave."

"Well, go on," a boy's voice said.

"Yeah, go on," another boy's voice said.

Midge and Larry moved out of their corner and looked up through the bars of the window. They saw three small figures, crawling on all fours, come into the little girl's cave.

"Hey, kids," Larry said softly.

"Hello, kids," Midge said.

The three figures stiffened and there was a common gasp.

"Don't be scared," Midge said.

"Where are you?" one of the boys said.

"Down here," Midge said. "In the cellar. You mustn't be frightened."

"We're not afraid," one of the boys said. "Maybe Izzy is."

"Is Izzy the little girl?" Midge said.

"Yeah."

"What's your name?"

"Bud."

"And what's his?"

"Mike," Bud answered. "What's yours?"

"Midge."

"What's his?" Bud asked.

"Larry."

"Good morning, kids," Larry said. "Nice of you to drop in."

"Thank you," Izzy said. "Do you live down there?"

Mike said patiently, "Nobody lives here anymore, don't you know that?" Then in surprise he said, "How'd you get down there?"

"We fell in," Midge said.

"Did you get hurt?" Izzy said.

"I got a bump on my head," Midge said.

"Aw," Izzy said.

"It's all right now," Midge said. "It doesn't hurt."

"Oh," Izzy said.

"How did you fall in?" Bud said.

"It was easy," Midge said. "But we don't like it down here. Will you help us get out?"

"Sure," Bud said.

"How?" Mike asked.

"Is your mother home, Bud?" Larry asked. "Or yours, Mike?"

"Ours isn't," Mike said. "She's workin' today."

"Is your father home?"

"We ain't got one," Mike said. "He's got one, though." He pointed to Bud with a touch of pride. "A mother, too."

"Is your mother home, Bud?"

"Yeah. Why?"

"Will you go and tell her about us? Tell her to call the police. They'll get us out of here."

The three children exchanged looks. Bud said, "My mother, she never listens to a thing I say."

"She will this time," Midge said. "Bud, will you do it right away? You see, we're hungry. We haven't had any breakfast."

"No breakfast?" Izzy said.

"No breakfast at all," Midge said. "So will you go home now and tell your mother? Tell her to call the police."

"Sure," Bud said.

"Will you go straight home?" Midge said.

"Sure," Bud said. "C'mon," he said to Izzy and Mike. "C'mon."

They crawled out of sight.

"Thank God," Larry said. "The mother will call the police. The kids will lead them to us. We could be out of here practically immediately."

"Oh," Midge said. "You haven't been happy here with me!"

"Happy as a lark," Larry said. He looked around their prison. "It isn't much, is it, but it's ours."

From his position on the corner he could see all the way up the block to Lexington Avenue, and down the Third Avenue side of the block to Ninety-fourth Street. He was watching for a young blonde girl and a tall man with a beard to come out of the inside of this block that was being demolished to make way for a new housing project. He had been warned that they might not come out together. Glancing at his watch, he saw that it had been only two and a half hours ago that he had taken over this post. It seemed longer.

The man he had relieved had been on the team tailing the couple when they had disappeared somewhere within the project. He had said that there was only one chance in a thousand that they could have got out before he and his partners had all four sides of the block under surveillance.

Since daybreak there had been two men inside looking for the couple. It was a mess in there, a million places to hide. Still, it was only a question of time before they found the two of them.

There were some boys playing stickball on the street. The man was glad to see that; it gave him an excuse, man watching game, to get out of the car parked near the corner and stretch his legs. He saw that the man on the corner of Lexington Avenue had the same idea. He couldn't see the man stationed at the corner of Third and Ninety-fourth, but he was there, and another man was at the corner of Lexington and Ninety-fourth. This guy with the beard, this Jacoby, didn't have a chance in hell of getting away. That was being seen to. This Jacoby must be a big one. He didn't know how the blonde girl figured in it. Nobody ever told him anything.

The stickball game broke up. He climbed back into his car. Settling himself behind the wheel, he saw three little kids on the sidewalk coming toward him. They hadn't been there a moment ago. He blinked and looked again, and they were still there. It was not an optical illusion. The only place they could have come from was the demolition project, but that seemed unlikely.

When the children got opposite the car, he leaned across the front seat and shouted his amusement at them. "Hey, you kids! Where the hell did you come from? Outer space?"

He hadn't meant to scare them, but they stopped dead, staring at him, eyes wide with fright. Then the tallest one, a boy, yelled, "Mike! Izzy! Run!"

"Hey," he said. "Hey, wait a minute!"

But they were off and running. The two boys had each grabbed one of the little girl's hands, and the little thing's feet were practically off the ground as they towed her along in full flight. They raced across the street and were lost to him behind the line of parked cars.

He had to laugh at the panic he had caused.

CHAPTER 8

THEY SAID they hadn't had any breakfast. It was almost twelve o'clock, they must be starving, Bud thought. He couldn't tell his mother about them, but he could take them something to eat. That was the least he could do.

Grownups, he knew, liked coffee for breakfast. But he didn't know how to make coffee. Even if he did, he didn't know what the man and the lady took in it. Sugar, milk, what? People liked eggs and toast for breakfast, too. He couldn't cook eggs, but he did know how to make toast. He looked in the breadbox. There were only a couple of crusts. He couldn't give them crusts, what would they think? He moved a kitchen chair over to the refrigerator, climbed up and looked into the fruit bowl on its top. Two oranges, three bananas. He would take them each an orange and a banana. He felt lousy about it. Two oranges, two bananas, big deal.

He put the fruit in a brown paper bag. Beggars can't be choosers, his grandfather often said, and remembering it made him feel a little better. Down the stairs, out of the house, he crossed the street so he wouldn't meet his mother coming home from the delicatessen. As he approached the corner of Third and Ninety-fourth, he thought of the man who had yelled at him and Mike and Izzy, the truant officer or building inspector or something. No, it was Sunday, no school, he couldn't be a truant officer, but whatever he was Bud knew he mustn't let the man see him go into the project. He stayed close to the drugstore on the corner and looked across Third. The man was still sitting there in the car, facing the other way. What was he doing, just sitting there? Well, Bud thought, he didn't know why adults did half the things they did.

He went to the opposite side of the street so he would be hidden from the man by the cars parked along the curb. Opposite the secret entrance he stopped and waited until a big truck was between him and the whatever the guy was. He ran across the street just in front of the big truck, and the driver swore at him.

"Up yours!" Bud hollered back. He wondered what that meant.

He hid between two cars that were parked in front of the secret entrance until a couple with a baby in a carriage got between him and the corner, then he darted across the sidewalk and into the vestibule. In another minute he was through that building and into the back yards of the block, and on his way to Izzy's cave. If only he had something more than two lousy oranges and two lousy bananas to give the lady and the man.

"How long has it been now?"

Larry looked at his watch. "Almost half an hour. We should have asked the kids where they lived. It could be one block away or twenty."

"It can't be far," Midge said. "Izzy is so little."

"That's right, Midge," he said. "Bud's mother and father probably just went out for a Sunday morning stroll. They'll be back any minute and he'll tell them about us."

"And the policemen who get us out of here will take us to your policeman friend and we'll tell him everything we've found out about Vic Jacoby and . . . Oh, Lord, I'd almost forgotten about Vic Jacoby. But I can well imagine you've been thinking about him."

"Frankly, yes."

"Anything special, or just general?"

"I've been thinking about him being in Europe. About your seeing him there."

"Yes?"

"Tell me about it, Midge."

"But I did. There isn't anymore to tell. I was in France. And I came up out of the water and started to walk along the beach . . . and there was Vic Jacoby."

"Go on."

"Well, that's really about all. There he was. I wasn't sure at first if I should even speak to him, he was sitting with a couple of men, but then he looked up and saw me and . . . and he seemed glad to see me! He came right over to me and said how about we take a walk on the beach? And we walked and talked, not about anything really, and we stopped in a place for a drink. Then all of a sudden he remembered he had an appointment and he was late. He walked to my hotel with me and left me there."

"And that's all?"

Midge hesitated. "Not quite all. He said he would call me, that we would have dinner together."

"But he didn't call?"

"No. I never heard from him again." She gave a little rueful laugh. "I guess he wasn't so darned glad to see me as I thought. But that doesn't help you, what I've been saying, does it?"

"No. But it doesn't change what I've been thinking, either."

"And that is?"

"That maybe it wasn't a couple of weeks ago here in New York that they first mistook me for Vic Jacoby. Maybe it was last summer in Europe that it happened first. I think they saw me there; they thought I was Jacoby. And they tried to kill me."

"Larry!" Midge said, her eyes wide with surprise. "You never said, you never told me . . ."

"I thought it was an accident. Everyone thought it was an accident. There was a smashup. We were on our way to the Barcelona airport. A friend of ours was leaving that night for New York. We were on our way to say good-by to him. . . ."

It all came back to him with a painful, shattering clarity. Enid at the wheel, driving much too fast with a kind of desperate wildness, Gerald beside her. He had been in the back seat with Nicole. The narrow road, a white, serpentine streak in the moonlight, flying beneath them. The wind whipping through their hair, lashing at their faces.

Nicole had been sad, mourning that Tom Bates was leaving them. She had needed a cigarette, she said, for comfort. He had had to loosen his safety belt to get at his lighter. He was holding it to the tip of her cigarette . . .

The explosion of the tire echoed in his mind. Once again he felt the car careen off the embankment, smash up over the stone guard and out into space. He felt himself hurled clear. Again he saw the car far below, plunging down onto the great boulders, bursting into flame. He could still see it laying there, burning brightly, turning the sea beside it into an orange glow. . . .

Midge said, "How awful. How ghastly. The others . . ."

"They were all killed," Larry said. "Enid and Gerald and Nicole, they were killed instantly. And if Nicole hadn't wanted a light, if I hadn't undone my belt . . ."

She stopped him. "No, don't say it, I don't want you to say it." She looked at him for a moment in silence, then she said, "Yes, I understand. You think it wasn't an accident, that it was their first attempt to kill Vic."

"I don't believe in coincidences like that, as big as that. Yes, I think they were trying to kill Vic Jacoby."

"You said a tire blew . . ."

"I thought that's what happened. I took for granted that it was an accident. But it could have been hit by a rifle. On that road, at that place, a blown tire meant almost certain death."

"But, Larry," she said, "they must have known that you didn't die, that you escaped?"

"Yes, I would think so."

"Then why did they ever let you leave Spain?"

"It wasn't their fault," Larry said grimly. "Don't blame them."

For three days after the accident he had hardly left his hotel room. What little he had eaten, what a great deal he had drunk had been sent up.

Late in the evening of the third day he made up his mind

to leave Cala Brava. He went down to the lobby, told them at the desk that he would be checking out in the morning, to forward any mail to him at the Hotel Menfis in Madrid. Then he went across to the bar.

It was quiet and, for the first time in the five weeks that he had lived in the hotel, almost deserted. Only a few scattered tables were occupied; the long, dark bar was empty. The customers, all regulars, sat drinking moderately, their voices subdued. There were none of the usual jokes, or the shrill laughter, or the calling out from one table to another. They glanced at Larry when he came in, then averted their eyes as if to spare him embarrassment. It was, he thought, as though he had no right to be here without Enid and Gerald and Nicole. It was still too soon after the tragedy; those three were still too much among them.

He sat alone at the bar and ordered a whiskey straight. In a moment a woman, sitting at a far table alone, rose and came to join him. She was Gail Borden, an American divorcée who had settled in Cala Brava to stretch her alimony into a more gracious living than it could afford her back home. He ordered a drink for her and for a while they sat in silence. Then she said abruptly, "You ought to get out of here, Larry."

He told her he was leaving in the morning.

"Where will you go?" she asked.

"Madrid."

"What will you do?"

"Take some pictures. I'll find a story there."

She shook her head doubtfully. "Are you sure you want to go to Madrid?"

"Why not?"

"It's too close," she said. "It's still Spain."

He smiled. "Where do you think I should go, Gail?"

"I think you should go home. How long has it been since you've been home?"

"Years, it seems."

"Then why don't you go home?"

He turned and looked at her. "Yes," he said suddenly, "why the hell don't I? I'll think about it."

"Don't think about it," she said. "Just go. Now. Tonight. You could catch the midnight plane from Barcelona."

"No," he said, "I can't do that. I have too many things to take care of."

"What, for instance?"

"Well, my car for one thing. And there's all my darkroom equipment to pack and ship . . ."

"I'll take care of everything," she said. "And I'll drive you to the airport. You can be on that plane tonight."

And, thanks to Gail Borden, he was. He was airborne, on his way to New York almost before he knew it. Certainly before Vic Jacoby's enemies had known it. That was why he had been able to get out of Spain alive. . . .

It was the purest of luck that a week ago the kids had found their secret cave. It was Izzy, actually, who found it, and she had a rare moment of glory. A bulldozer had pushed a pile of rubble up against and all over some sheet metal that was leaning against a house. Izzy had come across a hole in the pile. She had to go down on her hands and knees to crawl through it. Bud and Mike had seen her disappear, and they had crept in after her, and there was their secret cave, with a secret window with bars on it, opening on a secret celler. Izzy called it her secret cave; the boys had let her claim it as her personal property.

Bud crawled into the cave and over to the window. He couldn't see the lady and the man. "Hey," he said, "you still there?"

"Yes, Bud," the lady said.

He tore open the brown paper bag he was holding and thrust two oranges, two bananas through the bars.

"Here's some breakfast," he said.

"Why, thank you, Bud," the lady said. "Did you tell your mother about us? Did she call the police?"

Bud stared at them without answering.

"Bud," the man said quickly, "you did tell your mother, didn't you?"

"No," Bud said.

"Why not?" the lady said, and she sounded frightened.

"Well," he said, "she isn't home." And that's the truth, he thought to himself, she wasn't home. "She's gone to the store."

"But she'll be home soon, won't she?" the lady said.

"Sure."

"Oh!" the lady said, and now she sounded happy. "So the minute she gets home, you'll tell her, won't you? You'll tell her to call the police."

He knew he wasn't going to tell his mother, not as soon as she came home from the store, or ever, but he didn't want to tell the lady that.

"Sure," he said, and crawled away.

CHAPTER 9

TIM BRADY DROVE his taxi from six o'clock in the evening until two o'clock in the morning. Mrs. Tim Brady hated him to work those hours, but it was an indisputable fact that that was the time of the heaviest tipping. Tim rarely got to sleep until four A.M. and he usually woke up about noon. He had his breakfast while his wife and son had their lunch.

"Your turn to say grace," his mother said to Bud.

Bud took his turn at saying grace.

His father laughed and said, "Kid, you just broke the world's speed record for saying grace."

"I'm hungry," Bud said. "I'm starvin'."

"When you say grace," his mother said, "you should think what it means."

"What did you do all morning?" his father asked.

"Nothing much," Bud said.

"Where were you? The playground?"

"Yeah, the playground."

"Basketball?"

"Yeah, basketball. Get anyone famous last night, Pop?"

"Sure. The President and the Vice President and Mickey Mantle and Liz Taylor."

"You're kiddin' me!"

"Yeah, I'm kiddin' you. All I got was a bunch of twenty-five-cent tippers."

Mrs. Brady crossed the kitchen to the icebox and took a bowl of fruit down from the top of it. She looked in it and started to laugh.

"What's funny?" her husband asked.

"Bud, how could you be so hungry?"

"Huh?"

"Huh?" she repeated. "You mean, what did you say, Mother?"

"What did you say, Mother?"

"How can you be so hungry when you ate two oranges and two bananas since your breakfast? Or did you give them to somebody?"

"No, I didn't give them to anybody, honest!" Bud said.

"It would've been all right," his mother said.

"But I didn't!" Bud said. "Can I be excused, please?"

"Where you going so important?" his father asked. "Stick around. I never get to see you, it seems like."

"What do you want to see me for?" Bud asked.

"You're so good-looking," his father said. "You're a treat to the eye."

"You're kiddin' me," Bud said. "You're always kiddin' me."

Mrs. Fernandez hurried up out of the subway at Ninety-sixth Street. She almost never worked on a Sunday, but Mr. and Mrs. Porter were going on a trip and Mrs. Porter had a lot of extra washing and ironing and pressing for her to do.

It had taken her longer than she hoped. She had told the children that she would be home to make their lunch, and now it was almost half-past one. She stopped in at the place on Third Avenue and got some pizza. Even if Miguel and Isabelita had found themselves something, they could always eat some pizza. They would celebrate the extra money she had earned.

As she turned the corner into Ninety-fifth Street, she saw her two children. They were with that little whitey that lived downstairs. She frowned and walked faster.

The children did not see her until she was right beside them. Without a word she handed the pizza bag to Miguel and seized him by his left arm, Isabelita by her right arm and hustled them grimly away from Bud. The children were silent, too, until they were on the stairs to their apartment, then Isabelita began to sniffle. When the apartment door closed behind them, she burst into tears.

"I want to play with Bud!" she cried. "Why can't I play with Bud?"

"I've told you a thousand times, Isabelita!"

"Why can't I?"

"Because his father and mother don't think you and Miguel is good enough for him to play with!"

"Why?"

"Because he's white and you're not."

"I'm brown!"

"You're colored. You got to get that through your head. Before you get hurt something awful."

"Hurt? Hit?"

"I mean your feelings hurt. Miguel, you know what I'm talkin' about, don't you?"

"Maybe I do," Miguel said. "I don't know. Bud never

hurts our feelings."

"You've got to have pride! You shouldn't play with people don't think you're good as them. You got to have pride!"

"What's pride?" Isabelita asked.

"Miguel," his mother said, "you know what pride is."

"I guess so," Miguel said. "But Bud thinks we're as good as him."

"His folks don't! They practically hold their noses when they pass me on the stairs."

"Why do we live here?" Miguel asked.

"Because we got pride! It's a nicer place than further uptown and we got as much right as anyone to live here. Your father would turn over in his grave if he seen how some of our friends live."

"Why did we come here anyway?" Miguel asked. "Why didn't we stay in Ponce?"

"I promised your father I'd bring you and Isabelita to New York. He had hopes for you two. He thought it would be better for you in New York. In the United States. God forgive him. Now, let's be friends. I've got some pizza for us. A surprise!"

"I don't want any pizza," Miguel said.

"Me neither," Isabelita said. "I want to play with Bud."

"I wonder," Midge said, and by now speaking in a whisper had become automatic, "I wonder whatever can be keeping Bud's mother so long at the store."

"You know women," Larry said.

"What do I know?"

"Oh, they bump into each other at the store, they get to talking. One of them says to Bud's mother, stop in a minute,

I've got something I want to show you."

"And Bud's mother," Midge said, "not knowing we're down here, stops in to see what her friend has to show her."

"Wouldn't you?" Larry said. "Then after the friend shows Bud's mother her exciting new detergent and demonstrates how doubly clean and fluffy and sweet-smelling it gets her husband's and kids' filthy clothes, they open a bottle of champagne to celebrate Lever Brothers' latest victory."

"I'm sure that's what's happening," Midge said. "It happens all day long all over America. But by now Bud's mother is on her way home."

"By now," Larry said, "she is home. Bud is telling her about us."

"And by now," Midge said, "she is calling the police."

"Yes, at this very moment."

"And the police will be here before we know it," Midge said. "Do I look all right?"

"I've never seen you look better."

"When I was a kid," Midge said, "that was my trouble. I looked better with a dirty face." After another few minutes of waiting, of a total, shattering silence, Midge said, "I made a detergent commercial once. Want me to tell you about it?"

"Sure."

"No, I don't want to tell you about it," Midge said. "Where are those cops?"

"Don't forget they have to pick Bud up first, so he can show them where we are."

"That's right. And maybe the cops his mother called are the Canadian Mounties. I don't mean that. I know we'll be out of here soon."

"Sure we will," he said.

Silence fell upon them again. They sat stiff and still, backs pressed against the rough, cold wall of the cellar, straining to hear the sounds they waited for. The light, high voice of Bud, leading the expedition to them. The footsteps, the reassuring voices of the policemen. The clang of metal as the tin sheets that covered their window were toppled over. Light bursting through the small, barred window, and the faces of their rescuers looking down at them.

But the silence only lengthened and deepened. Try to think of something else, Midge told herself; forget about Bud and the police just for a few minutes, and there they'll be, the very moment you've stopped waiting for them.

"Larry," she said, "talk to me. Tell me what you're thinking about."

"I was thinking about Spain," he said. "About Vic Jacoby and Spain. I've remembered a strange thing that happened there. It was just before the accident, the same day that they were killed. That's probably why I never thought about it since. But now . . . well, now I have been thinking about it. And wondering. . . ."

It was early in the morning when he set out for Cadaqués. There was no direct road there from Cala Brava; he had to go inland to Figueras, then out through the mountainous wilderness back to the sea. The tiny crescent-shaped beach at Cadaqués was filled with exactly what he was looking for—girls in bikinis—and they were not camera-shy. His professional equipment told them that he was with either a newspaper or a magazine, and he had to practically fight them off.

After a good day's work he stopped in a bar off the beach for a beer. He was just finishing his second one when a tall, lanky American dropped down on the bench beside him. He picked the empty bottle off the table and read the label.

"San Miguel," he said. "This beer any good?"

"This beer is very good," Larry said.

"Then I'll have some," the man said, and beckoned a waiter. "And you'll have one with and on me."

"Delighted, sir."

"Call me Ed."

"Ed."

"Right the first time."

"Call me Larry."

"Larry."

They both laughed and raised fresh glasses to each other's health, wealth and wisdom.

Ed said, "You a tourist, Larry?"

"No, I'm working here at the moment."

"What's your line?"

"I take pictures. Travel magazine stuff."

"Taken any good pictures lately?"

"I think so. Girls in bikinis. On the beach here today."

"Is it hard to catch a girl in her bikini?"

"It's so easy it's dangerous. I was virtually mobbed. Girls wear bikinis so someone will take their pictures."

"You wouldn't say these girls were shrinking violets, I gather."

"You gather very well, no shrinking violets they. What's your line, Ed?"

"At the moment, tourista. My wife is shopping for post cards. I ran out on her. She chooses each post card as though it were a mink coat. Do you happen to know Figueras?"

"I've been through it often."

"Would it be a good place to spend the night? Ever notice a likely hotel?"

"As a matter of fact, I've noticed several."
"How are the post cards in Figueras, Larry?"
"Sorry, Ed, I couldn't say."
"I'll risk it. The little woman sends on the average of twenty-five post cards a day."
"Twenty-five, that's a lot of post cards, Ed."
"She has a wide circle of friends back home, a very wide and growing circle of friends. I find she didn't come over here to see Spain. She came over here, at my expense, to send post cards. Another beer, Larry?"
"Thanks, no, I've got to be on my way."
He said good-by to the lanky tourist, got in his car and drove up the steep, sinuous road out of Cadaqués. The sun had just begun to set; the sea reflected a sky turned salmon pink and coral. The road left the coast then and wound back to Figueras. A short distance outside the city he came to a small olive grove that spread down its terraces almost to the road. He pulled the car off the road and stopped.

"I parked there," he told Midge, "I've no idea why. There wasn't anyone around, not a house nor any building, there was nothing but that stand of olive trees. And I must have gone to sleep. I remember when I started off again, I turned on my lights. That's strange, you know . . ." His voice trailed to a stop.
"What is, Larry?" she asked.
"My falling asleep like that. I must have slept for at least an hour, maybe two."
"You were tired, maybe."
"No. Spending the day clicking a camera? No, that hadn't happened to me since I was a kid. A two-hour nap in the daylight! I even have trouble sleeping at night."

"But it didn't seem strange to you then, did it?"

"I don't know. I can't remember. I know I pulled off the road, but I don't know why. I can't remember falling asleep or waking up. It's all hazy, as though . . ."

"As though you'd been drugged?"

"Yes. As though I had been drugged."

"The American in the bar at Cadaqués?" Midge asked.

"Yes, I think so."

"He thought you were Vic. He put something in your drink."

"That seems to be the answer."

"Do you think he meant to kill you . . . kill Vic?"

He shook his head. "No. Not if all it did was to knock me out for an hour or two."

"Would he hope you would have an accident, go off the road, kill yourself?" She answered herself immediately. "No. That's not practical, not sure enough."

"No," Larry said. "I don't think Vic Jacoby was supposed to be killed. Not then. I think they merely wanted him out of the way for a couple of hours."

"But why?"

"Yes," he said. "Why?"

"Listen!" Midge said.

Larry listened, then nodded.

"It's Bud," Midge said, "and the police."

She started to rise, then sank down beside Larry again. She groped for and found his hand. The voices they had heard in the distance were coming closer. They faded, grew louder for a moment, then faded again. Whoever it was moving about the deserted project, they knew it wasn't Bud leading the police to their rescue. And they did not dare to raise their voices and find out who it was.

CHAPTER 10

THE PHONE RANG; he answered it.

Behind his broad back they called him The Cigar. Reluctantly, but in the line of duty, he removed his namesake from his mouth. It was Cuba's finest tobacco, delivered to him in New York by courier via Czechoslovakia. His superiors were glad to arrange that for him; he was a valuable man.

"Hello," he said into the phone.

"First, what time is it? My watch stopped."

"Half-past eight."

"I've had enough rest. I'm ready to go again. Bring me up to date."

"We had to call the ball game off for a while. A watchman spotted Megan this afternoon and threatened to make trouble. So they're still in there someplace, the two of them. We'll go back in as soon as the night watchman has a cup of coffee."

"Say that again?"

"The night watchman is a great coffee drinker. Makes his own. We got something into his bottle of instant that will not keep him awake."

"It will put him to sleep."

"He'll be out for a good eight hours. We got to wrap this thing up tonight. The workmen will be coming in tomorrow morning."

"We'll wrap it up tonight. What time you want me there?"

"The watchman should be out cold by ten o'clock."

"Right. I'll be there."

"Good."

He hung up, put the cigar back in his mouth. He was halfway through his next cigar when the call that he was waiting for came in. The night watchman had drunk his first cup of coffee. He was well taken care of; he would do no watching that night.

Bud had the television set turned on, but he wasn't watching it. He was thinking and worrying about the lady and the man down in the cellar. His father was at work; his mother was writing a letter at the kitchen table. He had to do something about the lady and the man.

"Bud," his mother said, stopping in the doorway, "I'm going out to mail this letter, then I'm going to sit with old Mrs. Mulligan downstairs for a while, poor thing."

"Okay."

"You'll go to bed at nine-thirty?"

"Yeah."

"You all right, Bud?"

"Huh? I mean, what did you say, Mother?"

"You been acting sort of funny today."

"No, I'm all right."

"Would you rather I stayed home with you?"

"No! You make me sound like a sis!"

"You're no sis, Bud." She laughed and said, "That's one thing about you, you're no sis."

"Thanks, Mom. You stay with Mrs. Mulligan as long as you want. I'll go to bed at nine-thirty."

"That's a good boy."

Bud went to the front window and stayed there until he saw his mother come out of the building and head down the street toward the mailbox on the corner. Then he ran through his bedroom and climbed out onto the fire escape. He went up one flight to Mike and Izzy's window. He knew they would be in their room; they had to go to bed at half-past eight. Their window was open about six inches; the room was dark.

"Hey, Mike," he whispered.

It was Izzy who whispered back. "Bud?" She tiptoed over to the window. Together they raised it a foot. They had done this often before.

"Is Mike in bed?" Bud asked.

"He's asleep. I have a stomach ache."

"Where's your mother?"

"Paintin' the kitchen."

"Wake Mike up, Izzy. But be real quiet."

In a moment the three of them were huddled together at the window. Bud said, "We got to do something about that lady and the man."

"Yeah," Mike said. "But what?"

"Tell our mothers about them?" Izzy said. "Like they said to?"

"Tell our mothers!" Bud said. "You crazy?"

"Yeah!" Mike said. "You crazy, Izzy?"

The boys looked at her in consternation.

"Listen, Izzy," Bud said. "Mike, you got to make her understand!"

"I understand," Izzy said quickly, frightened now by what she had said. "I didn't mean to say that, honest. I understand."

They were silent for a moment, remembering that terrible day; they would never forget it. It was the first time they had found the loose panel in the door and they had crawled inside where the buildings were being torn down. In the rubbish Izzy had found a bracelet with something that looked like diamonds all over it. It was pretty. Her mother had wanted to know where she got it. Had she taken it, stolen it out of the five and dime? Izzy and Mike had told her that she had found it, and to prove it they told her where, in the place where they were tearing the old buildings down.

Mrs. Fernandez had bawled them out something fierce for playing in such a dangerous place, and spanked them harder than they'd ever been spanked. She made them tell her who else had been with them. Then she had blamed it all on Bud. Mike and Izzy had never seen her so mad. She had gone right downstairs to see Bud's mother and she had screamed at her. It was the only time that the two mothers had ever spoken to each other and they were screaming. Bud's mother had told Mike and Izzy's mother that Bud's father had forbidden him to play with those kids of hers ever again.

The children had been frightened. It had been a week before they dared speak to each other even at school, but soon after that they were surreptitiously playing together. Before long the wonders and mysteries of the demolition project became irresistible to them, and they were playing there again. But they knew that they were committing a double crime against their parents. It was bad enough that they were playing in the project; it was even worse that they were playing together. That's why they knew they could never tell their parents about the lady and the man in the cellar. Their parents would kill them.

"At least," Bud said, "we can get them something more to eat. They must be starvin'."

"Yeah," Mike said, "let's get them something to eat."

"Your mother's in the kitchen," Bud said, "so I'll have to get them some stuff. But I gotta be awful careful. My mother saw the oranges and bananas was gone. Something else. It's cold tonight. They're gonna freeze to death down there."

"Yeah," Mike said. "We gotta get them some blankets, huh, Bud?"

"Yeah," Bud said, "two blankets. I can take the one off my bed. I make my own bed. My mother won't know it's gone. That's one."

"The lady can have mine," Izzy said. "That's two."

"Wait," Bud said. "You make your own bed?"

"No," Mike said.

"No," Izzy said.

"But we can start tomorrow," Mike said. "Like it was a surprise."

"Okay," Bud said. "Get me one of yours."

"I'll get mine," Izzy said.

"You gonna take the stuff to them now?" Mike said.

"Yeah, and I gotta hurry," Bud said. "My mother's just downstairs at Mrs. Mulligan's for a while."

"What about something to eat?" Mike asked.

"I'll find something," Bud said.

"Here," Izzy said, and pushed the roll of blanket into

Bud's hands.

"Thanks," Bud said.

"You're welcome," Izzy said.

Bud crept down the fire escape and stripped the blanket off his bed. In the kitchen he made four peanut butter and jelly sandwiches. He filled an empty quart beer bottle with water. He remembered he had half a chocolate bar in his room. Fixing the lock on the hall door so that he could get back in, he tiptoed down the stairs. As he passed Mrs. Mulligan's door, he heard her old phonograph going. A man named John McCormack was singing. He was Mrs. Mulligan's favorite singer. Right now he was singing a song called "My Wild Irish Rose."

When he got to the corner of Third and Ninety-fifth, Bud thought of the man in the car that had yelled at the three of them. He was sure the man wouldn't still be there, the inspector or plainclothesman or whatever he was, but Bud sneaked a look just to make sure. In the glow of the street lights and store windows he saw that the same car was there, but there was a different man in it. Something was going on, Bud thought, but he couldn't figure out what it could be. Maybe it was something about pot or dope or race riots.

It being dark now, it would be easier to get into the vestibule without the man seeing him. Maybe. He couldn't be sure about that, but he hid in the hallway inside the secret entrance and waited, and the man didn't come prying around so he felt safe so far, but it was scary kind of, it was so dark. He wished he had a flashlight. No, he couldn't use a flashlight. Somebody might see him. When he got outside, in the back yards, he found he could see better, and soon he was crawling into the cave and over to the cellar window.

"Hey, lady," he said. "Hey, mister."

"Bud!" the lady said.

"Yeah, it's me. You like peanut butter and jelly sandwiches?"

"Love them," the lady said.

"Great," the man said.

"You're very thoughtful, Bud," the lady said.

"And here's some water." He pushed the sandwiches and the bottle through the window bars. "And I got two blankets for you. Are you cold?"

"Yes," the lady said. "You're very, very thoughtful, Bud."

He had to partly unfold the blankets to slip them through the bars. The lady kept talking to him all the while. "Bud," she said, "it's nice of you, but you have to tell somebody about us. Is it because you're afraid, Bud? Look, if you can't tell your mother, if you're afraid to tell your mother and father that you were playing here, there must be somebody you can tell. . . ."

"No," Bud said. "They would tell my mother and father and they . . ."

"Bud," the man said, "your mother and father would be glad that you got us out of here. . . ."

"Not my father!" Bud said. "My father would kill me!"

He backed away from the window and crawled quickly out of the cave. The lady and the man were still calling to him, but softly, as he stumbled away in the darkness. He was almost back to the house where the secret entrance was when the ray of a flashlight hit him full in the face.

"Hey! Hey, kid!" a man said, and he sounded surprised.

Bud raced around a hill of bricks, a pile of lumber. This part of the project he knew, and he knew that there was a bulldozer over there. He groped his way to it and crawled underneath it. The light came around the pile of lumber.

Another man said, "What's going on?"

"A kid! A little kid!"

"In here, now? You're seeing things, Max."

"No. A little boy."

"Come off it!"

"He's around here someplace."

Two flashlights flickered over the bulldozer. If they found him, Bud thought, if they took him home and told on him, his father would be fit to be tied. His father had this thing about him that his mother called his God-awful temper. She meant that he got mad easy. And she was right about that. His father would beat the hell out of him.

"Where could that kid have got to?" he heard one of the men say.

"If there ever was a kid," the other man said, and laughed. "In case it's slipped your mind, we're not looking for a kid. We're looking for Jacoby."

The voices and the beams of light moved away. Bud waited awhile to make sure it was safe to come out from under the bulldozer. Then he waited in the vestibule until some people came between him and the corner where the man sat in the car. He was sure he got across the street and past the corner without the man seeing him.

On the way up the stairs of his house, he stopped at Mrs. Mulligan's door. John McCormack was finished singing. He heard his mother and Mrs. Mulligan talking.

He put on his pajamas, then climbed the fire escape up to Mike and Izzy's window. He whispered to them, but they were asleep. Tomorrow he would tell them what had happened. Besides, he had to get to bed before his mother came home.

He just made it. He had to pretend he was asleep when she came in to look at him. It took a long time, though, to really go to sleep; he was all jumpy inside.

CHAPTER 11

SINCE THE FLOOR had shuddered open beneath them and they had been hurtled down into the cellar, this had been their worst hour. They had heard the man's voice shout at Bud, then they had heard nothing more. They didn't know if the man had caught Bud, if Bud had been frightened into confessing what he had been doing in the project at this time of night. At any moment they expected the glare of a flashlight to come through the window. They huddled in a corner, hiding themselves the best they could, knowing that it was a desperate, futile action. If Bud had been forced to inform on them, they knew there was no escape.

But the minutes dragged past, until an hour was gone, and nothing happened. It was obvious now that Bud was not going to help in their rescue, but at least he had not hurt them. They blessed him for that. And now each hour that safely passed would bring them closer to freedom. In the morning the workmen would arrive.

At last they dared to leave their inadequate hiding place in the corner. When Midge discovered that her teeth were chattering and realized, with pride, that it was not from fright now but from the cold, she remembered the blankets. Then, reasonably warm, she realized that she was ravenous and remembered the sandwiches. She had finished one and was groping for her second when she found there were three left.

"Larry," she said, "you'd better eat something."

He did not answer.

"Larry!" she said.

"Yeah?"

"What is it, Larry? What are you thinking about? You're remembering something."

"Yes. I've remembered something . . . something strange."

"About Vic Jacoby."

He nodded in the darkness. "Yes. And I think it might explain a little more about Vic Jacoby and me."

The core of the set had been lolling about the shallow end of the pool, basking and tanning in the August sun. As was their custom, they had convened approximately at noon to supervise the cure of each other's hangovers. They were playing their favorite game of the moment; it was known as thinking the worst of people.

"See that chap," Gerald said, "to the left of the diving board?"

"With the atrocious nose?" Enid asked.

"That's the one," Gerald said.

"What about him?" Nicole asked, and giggled.

"Gathers little children around him in parks," Gerald said, "reads dirty books to them."

"His wife writes the books," Larry said.

"I suppose," Enid said, "they have no children of their own."

"Hardly," Gerald said.

"They could adopt," Enid said, "and save him the trouble of going to the park."

Behind him a voice said casually, "Hey, Larry, do you happen to know a guy named Tom Bates? Tall, good-looking fellow, smart as a whip?"

Larry rolled over on his back and looked up at the man who stood behind him. He was a good-looking fellow, tall with clean, even features and a blond, thick crew cut and fair skin that was still unburned by the Spanish sun.

"Tom!" Larry said. "Well, I'll be damned!"

They shook hands and pounded each other's shoulders. "Where did I come from, huh?" Tom said. "What am I doing here?"

"Yes!" Larry said. "I'll be damned. Tom Bates!"

"First," Tom said, "introduce me to the beautiful girls. Don't bother about the gent."

Gerald laughed and said, "This one is Enid, and she's mine."

Tom pointed to Nicole. "Can I have that one?"

"Yes," Nicole said. "My name is Nicole, darling."

"Oh," Tom said to Larry, "so she isn't yours."

"No," Larry said. "I'm not good-looking, smart as a whip. Tom, what the hell, tell me! Did you know I was here, how did you find me, what?"

"I ran into Teddy Smith in St Louis . . ."

"Yes, Teddy was here for a couple of weeks."

"And he told me about the life you were leading here. Sun and sand and girls and the beautiful Mediterranean and girls and cheap booze and girls. So I said what's good enough for

Larry Towers is good enough for me. I quit my job and here I am."

"I'm so glad, darling," Nicole said.

"You quit your job?" Larry said.

"I was fed up with St Louis."

"What do you do, darling?"

"I'm a press agent, publicity, public relations." He turned back to Larry. "And when I spend all my money on Nicole here in Spain, I'll go home and get some kind of job on the West Coast."

"No, not on the West Coast, darling," Nicole said. "Paris."

"Anything you say, darling. How do you get a drink in Spain? Who do you have to know?"

"Me," Nicole said. "Only me."

She called a waiter; she translated Tom's order to him and instructed him to bring more drinks all around. She installed Tom in the chair next to hers and proceeded to tell him all about herself, beginning with the fact that at the moment she was not married, not in any way involved with any certain man, that she was, at the moment, completely free.

A synthetic blonde with a weary face but a magnificent figure sat down on a lounge nearby. Larry had never seen her before; she was a newcomer. In a whiskey tenor she said, "Would one of you boys smear some of this sun-tan muck on my back, if you aren't busy?"

"Gerald is busy," Enid said.

"So is Tom," Nicole said.

"Larry," Gerald said, "you win."

Larry rose and sat next to the blonde. "It looks," he said, "as if the pleasure is mine."

"Don't enjoy it too much," she said. She handed him the bottle of lotion, stretched out on her stomach, undid the strap of her bikini. "Put it on thick, will you? This sun is like a violet ray."

Larry went to work on her shoulders. "Perhaps I should introduce myself," he said. "Larry Towers."

"Glad to meet you, Mr. Towers. Rub it in good. Mrs. Kaufman."

"I don't recall," Larry said, "seeing you around before, Mrs. Kaufman."

"I just got here this morning."

"Oh. Is that yellow Ferrari yours?"

"That's right."

"Beautiful."

"Thanks. Lower, please, Mr. Towers; all the way down. Incidentally, they tell me the nearest good garage is in Gerona. Is that right?"

"I'm afraid so. I wouldn't trust a car like that to any garage around here."

"How long will it take me to get to Gerona? Forty minutes?"

"Just about that," Larry said. "Can you reach the back of your legs all right, Mrs. Kaufman?"

"That's quite a sense of humor you got there, Mr. Towers. Yes, I can reach the back of my legs all right."

"Well, then, I guess that about does it, Mrs. Kaufman."

"Thanks, Mr. Towers."

"Anytime, Mrs. Kaufman."

Larry went back to his chair, picked up his new drink.

Nicole said, "Tom is telling me you went to school together."

"I don't remember Tom ever actually going to school," Larry said, "but we were there at the same school together."

Nicole turned back to Tom. "Darling, did you not study?

Bad boy."

"Tom," Larry said, "are you going to stay here? Have you checked in yet?"

"Not yet."

"Tom is not checking in here!" Nicole said. "Are you, darling?"

"Anything you say, dear. Everything you say. Where am I checking in?"

"I am at a pension on the mountainside. A spectacular view of the sea! Reasonable rates. I will arrange for you to have a room next to mine. Yes, darling?"

"You said it, dear."

"It will be heaven," Nicole said.

"Heaven," Tom Bates said, "will never be like this."

"The sun-tan woman," Midge said, "and the American who talked to you in the bar at Cadaqués . . . they both used the word violet."

"That's right. He talked about shrinking violets. She said the sun was like a violet ray. That must have been some kind of a signal. And after that they both mentioned the name of a town, and a number. That would have meant something. A code, possibly a rendezvous, something."

"But mightn't it . . . No, it couldn't possibly have been a coincidence."

"I wouldn't think so," Larry said. "I think it looks as though Roma Tyler was right about Vic Jacoby, that he was in espionage. Those two people were probably agents, and they thought they were establishing a contact with Vic."

"Good Lord!" Midge said, and shook her head in awe. "Even Vic's own people mistook you for him."

CHAPTER 12

THERE WERE FOUR LOVES in Mack Rowley's life—his wife, his son, his daughter, and the crane with its swinging ball. When he was a kid, he wouldn't go to the ball games with his pals; he would go to the biggest demolition job in the five boroughs of Greater New York and watch his hero, the crane operator—any crane operator—knock down old buildings with that swinging iron ball. Let others grow up to be priests, doctors, lawyers, hackies and doormen. From the age of seven Mack knew that when he got big, he would swing that beautiful iron ball and make those walls come tumbling down. It hadn't been easy. There are only so many cranes and iron balls in action. He had got his first job in the sticks in New Jersey. It had taken him six years to work his way into a permanent position in New York, the big time, where you get the largest crowds and the best pay.

Saturday and Sunday were wasted days to Mack, but at last it was Monday morning again. He found himself taking the steps up out of the subway two at a time, and he laughed out loud in sheer, exuberant joy. Then, at the entrance to the project, he got his usual feeling of dread. Something had happened to his crane in his absence, some woe had befallen it. But no, as always, there it stood, tall, proud, in all its glory. He patted one of its mammoth tires and bid it a good morning. He hadn't realized how early it was; no one seemed to be around yet.

Tossing his lunch box up into the cabin, he planned his day's work. There were four and a half buildings still standing here on the Ninety-fourth Street side. In a couple of hours he could easily knock down the half building and get a good start on its neighbor before lunch. He could finish it off, and the next one maybe before quitting time. Man, oh, man, would walls come tumbling down this day! He climbed up into the cab, settled himself there.

"Hey, Mack!"

He looked down. "Good morning to you, Fatso," he said.

"Come down outa there!" Fatso said.

"What the hell!" Mack said. "I got work to do!"

"Not yet you don't!"

"What the hell!" Mack said. "What gives?"

"Come down outa there and I'll tell you."

Mack sighed and climbed down out of the crane.

"We," Fatso said, "got a grievance against the company. It's a walkout, a work stoppage, a pullout."

"What's our beef?" Mack said. "I got no beef. I'm happy."

"They laid off Ricco."

"Why?"

"Drinking. Mueller claims he was drunk Friday afternoon."

"Was he?"

"He says no. He only had a quart of beer for lunch, he

says. But Mueller says he was loaded and endangering the lives of his fellow workers."

"Nuts!" Mack said. "Ricco never does enough work on the job to endanger anyone."

"There's that, too," Fatso agreed. "Ricco is nothing on the job. Mueller has been out to get him canned for a long time."

"The union should never have let Ricco in!"

"Yeah, but once the union lets a man in, they got to stick by him. What's a union for? Ricco, he's got a wife and four kids."

"So he shouldn't drink."

"That's maybe why he drinks," Fatso said, and laughed.

"What's happening now?"

"The union is in conference with Mueller and Ricco."

"Hell!" Mack said. "I got work to do! How long could it take? How long might we be out?"

"It could take hours, or it could take days or weeks or months," Fatso said, and laughed again. "Eventually we might have to call the Mayor in."

Larry held his watch up to the dusky shaft of light; it was twenty-five minutes past eight. Again, as he had done every few minutes for the last hour, he hoisted himself up to the window and listened. He could hear the hum of cars, the roar of trucks and buses on the surrounding streets. But within the block there was silence; there were none of the sounds that he had been waiting all night to hear—the sounds of men at work, the men who would get Midge and him out of here.

Sometime during the night he and Midge had cleared a small section of the concrete floor of the fallen debris and rolled up in Bud's blankets. They were too exhausted to even try to speak, to make the little jokes meant to cheer each other up. They huddled together in silence. At last Midge's measured breathing told him that she had mercifully fallen asleep.

There had been no sleep for him. Early in the night there had come to his mind a nagging, dragging thought of something, something unknown, that was buried in his past. He had the feeling that something had happened to him, something that was important to him now, and for some reason he had blacked it out. He wondered if it had happened, whatever it was, in the last few years, in Spain or Italy or France, or before that, possibly when he was working in Chicago. Or did it go further back than that, all the way back, perhaps, to his boyhood in California?

And why, he asked himself incredulously, why had this phantom remembrance suddenly become so important? Why, at this ungodly time, here in this ghastly trap into which he and the girl had fallen, why now of all times should it hover over him, needling him, bugging him, begging to be remembered? Carefully, painfully, as though he were undergoing a deep and disturbing analysis, he forced his mind back through time. If he could relive his life, day by day, step by step, he would, pray God, come upon this secret that was buried in his subconscious, understand it and lay it to rest.

He thought back on his weeks in New York, from Midge's and his search for information about Vic Jacoby just the night before back through the weeks he had spent hiding in the hotel off Union Square, waiting futilely for the police to help him. He thought of the attempt on his life on the lonely country road, of his first meeting with Midge, of his plane trip from Barcelona to New York. He relived those harrowing days following the accident and the death of Nicole and Enid and Gerald. When his mind came to the accident itself, it balked and remained there.

The feeling came over him that it was because of the accident, the shock of the sudden, simultaneous deaths of his three friends, that this thing he sought was eluding him. The shock of his loss had knocked something from his mind, something that involved the four of them and that, until now, he had not wanted to remember. And now it seemed to be hovering on the threshold of his consciousness, but there it stayed, torturing and tantalizing him. In spite of his struggle he could not make it come out of the darkness and reveal itself to him.

The first daylight had found its way through the window without his noticing. When at last he did see it, he moved quietly, being careful not to wake Midge, to stand under the window and look at his watch. It was a few minutes before six. As the next two hours crawled past, Midge slept on, and he thanked God that at least this was one vigil she was spared. He thought with pleasure that he would let the sound of the men at work outside their window waken her. She would wake up just in time to be rescued. Then the hands of his watch had crept past eight, to quarter after, to half past, and the workmen had not arrived. At nine there was still silence inside the block.

Midge sat up a few minutes later. She had got to her feet, seen the light filtering through the window and said in delighted surprise, "It's morning!"

"Yes," he said. "Good morning."

"What time is it?"

He hesitated; he couldn't bear to tell her the truth. "A little after six," he said.

"Glory be!" she said. "They'll be here in less than two hours."

"That's right," he said. "Less than two hours."

But she had heard something in his voice. "Larry," she said, "something's gone wrong with the workmen. . . . What time is it, really?"

Now he had to tell her the truth. "Ten minutes after nine, Midge."

"Ten after nine," she said slowly. "Ten after nine and they aren't here?"

"They may be working at the other end of the project," he said, "doing something we can't hear."

"Oh, Larry, you don't believe that! My God, they're tearing down houses! We would hear them! Oh, God, what is it? They've stopped work on this project, they won't be here, they aren't coming . . ."

For the first time she cracked. A whimper of despair broke through her lips and her shoulders shook with long, dry sobs. Larry pulled her to him, held her very close, comforting her and damning himself for getting her into this.

"Yesterday morning," the man said, "Krebs saw three kids pop up on the sidewalk. They could only have come out of the project. Last night I found a kid in there. He got away from me. He might have been one of the kids Krebs saw. When they ran away from him, this kid yelled two names. Mike and Izzy."

"Mike and Izzy," the other man said.

"Maybe if you looked and asked around the neighborhood, you could locate them."

"And through them I could maybe find the boy you saw last night."

"That's what I had in mind."

"And I could find out what the kid was doing in there last night."

"You dig me."

"A little kid like that doesn't go into a place like that after dark just to play."

"It doesn't seem so to me."

"I'll do my best to find this kid."

"Do better than that."

"You think he might know where Jacoby and the girl are. Well, if he does, I'll see to it that he tells me."

"You and me. Only be careful not to scare the kids, make them afraid to talk."

"I don't scare kids. I like kids, kids like me."

Forty minutes later he walked into a small store near the corner of Third Avenue and Ninety-fifth Street, the third store of its kind he had been in. It sold newspapers, magazines, paperback books. Cigars, cigarettes. Stationery, funny and serious birthday and anniversary and get-well cards. Ballpoint pens and pencils. Penny, nickel and dime candy, comic books for children of all ages. The proprietor turned away from a pile of yesterday's newspapers he had just counted and said, "What can I do for you?"

"Maybe you can do me a favor."

"Hope so," the proprietor said, "good for business."

"You're right, and to prove it, give me a couple packs of Trues. The blues."

"True blues? No sooner said than done." The proprietor gave him the cigarettes, rang up the price on his cash register and gave the customer his change. "Now for the favor I might do you."

"Well, my little boy is sick and . . ."

"Sorry to hear that," the proprietor said. "Nothing serious, I hope."

"He had appendicitis."

"Acute?"

"Acute enough to have it out. But he's back from the hospital now and . . ."

"Glad to hear it," the proprietor said. "I got a get-well card over there especially suitable for appendicitis. It's a howl."

"I'll have one of those, but what I really want is . . . you see, my boy has a birthday coming up and . . ."

"I got some really funny birthday cards over there," the proprietor said. "Real riots."

"I'll look into those, too. But what I'm trying to say is . . ."

"And I'm not letting you say it," the proprietor said. "Excuse me, go ahead."

"My kid being sick in bed, the wife and me would like to cheer him up with a little party."

"A birthday party," the proprietor said, nodding.

"That's what we had in mind. Now, he's got a couple of friends in school he especially wants to invite to his party, but he doesn't know their last names or where they live. He only knows them as Mike and Izzy."

"Mike and Izzy," the proprietor said. "Colored kids?"

"Well, yes. You going to throw me out of your store?"

"No, the colored kids I don't mind, some I even like, cute," the proprietor said. "But that's beside the point."

"Yeah, I'm hoping you can tell me where Mike and Izzy live."

"They come in here off and on," the proprietor said, and he laughed in advance at the joke he was about to make. "But I don't make deliveries to Mike and Izzy, so I don't know exactly what house they live in. But it's around the corner somewhere on Ninety-fifth. I don't know their last names, but you shouldn't have any trouble finding them. I understand that they're the only colored kids on the block."

"Hi, Mom," Bud said.

"Hi, Bud. How was school?"

"Okay."

His mother laughed and said, "When you say okay, you don't mean okay. You mean it's no good."

"Who likes school?" Bud said. "Not even the teachers. You can tell."

His mother laughed again. He wished his mother wasn't in the kitchen. The lady and the man in the cellar hadn't had anything to eat since last night. His mother was ironing. There was still a big pile of dampened stuff on the table for her to do; she was going to be in the kitchen a long time. He couldn't get anything for the man and the lady to eat or drink until she got out of the kitchen. And after she finished the ironing, she would probably start cooking dinner. She was going to be in the kitchen a long time, until they ate and she washed the dinner dishes and maybe even mopped the floor.

"What are you going to do now, Bud?"

"Can I go to the playground?"

"Basketball?"

"Yeah, maybe. Something. Okay, Mom?"

"There's that okay again."

"What should I say instead?"

"Well, like yes, Mother! Like you mean it!"

"Yes, Mother! Can I go now?"

"Okay," his mother said, and laughed.

Bud went out of the kitchen, through the front door to the hall door. He opened it and slammed it shut from the inside. He sneaked back through the front room to his room. Out the window, up the fire escape. Izzy was lying on her bed, looking at a comic book. She was reading it out loud to herself.

"Izzy," Bud whispered, "your mother home?"

"No, she's workin'."

"Where's Mike?"

"Gettin' his hair cut."

Bud climbed through the window. "I gotta take the lady and the man something to eat, but my mother's in the kitchen. You got anything?"

"I don't know," Izzy said. "Oh, there's some brownies my mother made for us after school."

"You pretend you and Mike ate them. Tell your mother how good they were."

"And there's our milk."

"Okay."

Izzy got him the brownies and milk. "Can I go with you?"

"No."

"Okay. Say hello to the lady. And the man."

The same car was still parked up at the corner and there was another man sitting in it. Crazy, Bud thought, how come? He waited for the right moment to get across the street and into the vestibule without the man seeing him. Inside the project it was absolutely quiet. Nobody was working. Bud couldn't understand it but he didn't waste any time trying to figure it out. He got clear to the cave without seeing anyone or having to hide from anyone.

"Hey, lady; hey, mister," he said.

The two of them came up to the window. They said hello to him.

"Here's some brownies and some milk," he said.

"Thank you," the lady said.

"Did the blankets keep you warm?" Bud said.

"Yes," the lady said. "Thank you."

"You're welcome," Bud said. "Good-by."

"Wait!" the man said. "Bud, listen . . ."

"I can't! I gotta go!"

The man put his hand through the bars and grabbed Bud's wrist. "Listen to me, Bud," he said. "Somebody is trying to hurt us. To kill us. Do you understand that, Bud?"

"Someone is tryin' to kill you?" Bud said. "Really tryin' to kill you?"

"Yes, Bud."

"Who?"

"Gangsters," the lady said.

"Are you gangsters?" Bud asked.

"No," the lady said.

"I don't guess you'd tell me if you were," Bud said.

"Does she look like a gangster?" the man asked.

"No," Bud said.

"And gangsters don't wear beards," the lady said. "You watch television, don't you? You ever see a gangster with a beard?"

"No," Bud said.

"So you'll help us, won't you, Bud? Help us get out of here?"

"I can't!" Bud said, and he tried to pull away, but the man's hand was tight on his wrist.

"Bud," he said, "you don't have to tell your mother or your father. Tell someone else. . . . Don't you have an older friend?"

"No, I don't have any older friends. I don't like older friends."

"Do you know the policemen on your block?" he asked.

"Which one?"

"Which one do you like best?"

"I only like Red," Bud said. "We call him Red. He lets us."

"Will you tell him about us?" the lady said. "And bring him here, show him where we are?"

"I might," Bud said, considering the possible danger. "Maybe. You'll get killed if I don't? Really killed?"

"Yes," she said. "The men who are trying to kill us are right here, right inside the project looking for us. If they find us, they will kill us."

"Then I better hurry," Bud said, "and tell Red."

"Please hurry, Bud," she said.

The man let go of his wrist. He said, "Thanks, Bud."

"Okay," Bud said. "I'll hurry."

He crawled to the edge of the sheets of tin and peeked out. No one was in sight. On his way back to the house with the secret door in it he thought he heard someone behind him and he hid, but it was a false alarm. As he went into the empty rear basement of the house, he heaved a sigh of relief.

Just inside the doorway a hand fell on his shoulder.

"Hello, son," a man said.

Bud squirmed and tried to pull away. "Let me go!"

"I'm not going to hurt you, son," the man said. "You have fun playing in here?"

"I promise never to come in here again! Let me go!"

"Take it easy, son," the man said, and smiled at him. "Don't be scared."

Bud looked up at the man. He was still smiling; he looked friendly. Bud stopped being scared. The man didn't look as though he would hurt him or tell his father on him. Bud tried to smile back up at the man, as though it wasn't wrong of him to be here.

"You work here, mister?" he said.

"Not exactly," the man said. "You play here all the time, don't you?"

"Not all the time," Bud said. "Only every once in a while."

"Maybe you can do me a favor," the man said.

"Sure. What?"

"I'm looking for a couple of friends of mine," the man said. "A girl and a fellow with a beard. They came in here to look around yesterday and I can't find them. I'm afraid maybe they got themselves in trouble, got themselves locked in someplace where they can't get out maybe. You know how that happens. Maybe it happened to you sometime."

Bud could hardly believe his good luck. He didn't have to find Red the Cop and tell him. Here was a friend of the man and the lady in the cellar. All he had to do was take him to the window and in no time the man and the lady would be out of the cellar. They would be all right. They could get police protection, you call it, from the gangsters.

"Yeah," Bud said, "there's a lady and a man got themselves where they can't get out. Mike and Izzy and me found them."

"Can you lead me to them, son?"

"Sure," Bud said. "C'mon!"

CHAPTER 13

"IT STINKS," Mack the crane operator said to his wife over the phone. "I could kill that Ricco."

"Whose side you on?" his wife said. "You sound anti-union."

"A union shouldn't stand up for drunks, for God's sake!"

"You're just sore," she said, "because you aren't swinging that ball." She laughed. "My big little boy sure loves to swing that ball, knock down dem walls, tote dat barge."

"Go ahead, make fun of me. A man takes pride in his job and his wife makes fun of him. I worked like hell to get where I am."

"I know you did, sweet. Look, why don't you relax and come home? It's getting pretty late in the day for them to settle this thing."

"They might get it settled any minute now," he said. "I could still get a couple good hours' work in. Besides, what the hell would I do at home?"

She giggled. "I'll have Billy build a house out of his blocks. And you can knock it down."

"Go to hell," he said.

She giggled some more. "I love you," she said.

"Look," he said, "I'll hang around here for another half hour, okay? And if they haven't patched it up by that time, the hell with it. I'll come home, okay?"

"Okay," she said, and hung up.

Bud, with the guy right behind him, went through the back-yard doorway of the secret entrance house; he took two or three steps, stopped suddenly and turned around to face the guy.

"Hey, mister!"

"What is it, son?"

"For helpin' save them, will I get my picture in the newspaper?"

"You bet! You'll be a hero! You and Mike and Izzy will all get your pictures in the paper."

"No!" Bud said. "My father will beat the hell out of me!"

"You mean for playing in here? Because it's dangerous? No, don't worry about your father, son. He's going to be proud of you! Saving the lady and the man, your mother and father they'll be real proud of you!"

"Yeah, maybe," Bud said. "But there's something else."

"What?"

"I'm not allowed to play with Mike and Izzy. And they aren't allowed to play with me. I'm white and they're colored kids." Bud was almost crying. "My father would beat the hell out of me! And I don't know what Mrs. Fernandez would do to Mike and Izzy! You gotta promise our pictures don't get in the paper. My father reads all the papers. In his cab. You gotta promise."

"Okay, son, it's a promise."

"Or our names either!"

"Or your names. It's a promise."

"And you won't tell anyone at all? If my father ever finds out . . ."

"Son, this will be our secret. Look, I won't even tell the lady and the man. You can just point out the place they are and then you can beat it on home. Nobody will ever know but you and me. Okay?"

"Okay," Bud said with a great sigh of relief. Everything was all right again. He could help the lady and the man without getting himself and Mike and Izzy in trouble. He grinned up at the guy. "Hey," he said, "were you in here yesterday morning? Lookin' for your friends? I think it was you I saw."

"It could've been me. I was here."

"Yeah, I saw you. Us kids hid from you."

"That right? Let's get moving, shall we, son? My friends must be getting pretty anxious to get out of there."

"Yeah!" Bud said. "Will they be glad to see you!"

As he got moving, with the guy right behind him, something scary stirred in his mind. Would the lady and the man be glad to see this guy? Bud remembered what the lady had said, about the men trying to kill them being right inside here, looking for them. She said they might find them any minute.

All of a sudden Bud got a sick feeling in his belly. This guy could be one of the men trying to kill them. He could be, Bud thought; he didn't look like any friend the lady would have. She was so nice and he was kind of rough, tough sort of. He could be one of the gangsters she said was after them, Bud thought, and here he was leading him right to the lady and the man. It was all Bud could do to keep from breaking into a run. Just in time he realized that the guy would catch him easy. He knew he couldn't run, but he had to do something. It would be his fault if the lady and the man got killed. He thought with all his might.

"Wait a minute," Bud said, stopping and looking all around. "Let me see."

"You're not sure where you're going, son?"

"Yeah, I know, now I know. Everything keeps changin' in here. C'mon, it's this way. I just got mixed up for a minute."

"Don't be nervous, son; just take it easy."

"Yeah," Bud said.

He led the guy as far away from the right place as he could, toward a house that was on the opposite side of the block. Mike and Izzy and he had explored it, and on the third floor they had found a door that they couldn't get open. They tried and tried, dying to know what was inside, but the door wouldn't budge.

"Boy!" Bud said. "Will they ever be glad to see you!"

"You bet they will," the man said. "You sure you know where you're going?"

"There!" Bud said. "That house there."

The man looked at the house where Bud was pointing. It had been gone through thoroughly yesterday and again this morning and it had been empty. But it was possible, of course, that Jacoby and the girl had been able to elude them by moving from place to place. Difficult, but possible. In fact, it seemed the only explanation.

"That's where they are, son?" he said.

"That's it," Bud said. "Up on the third floor there's a door won't open. You'll find them easy."

"Thanks, son."

"Can I beat it on home now?" Bud asked.

"Sure, thanks a million."

Bud tried not to run too fast. Just once he looked back over his shoulder. The guy was going into the basement of the house, the wrong house. The man and the lady, Bud thought, would be all right for a little while longer maybe. But he better find Red the Cop as soon as he could.

The three small girls playing jump rope took up the entire width of the sidewalk. When the man stopped near them, they thought, naturally enough, that he wanted to get by. On the next miss they moved over to the curb, but he stayed where he was. He smiled at them.

"Hello, there!"

"Hello," two of them said. The third had promised her mother she would never speak to strangers.

"Having fun?"

"Yes."

"Do you know a little girl named Izzy?"

"Izzy Fernandez?" one of them said.

"Yeah, could be," he said. "Do you know where she lives?"

"That's her sittin' over there on the steps."

"Thank you."

The three little girls went back to skipping rope. The man crossed the street. He sat down on the steps beside Izzy. Izzy wasn't concerned about him; she kept on humming, sometimes she would sing a few words.

"Hello," the man said.

"Hello," Izzy said. "Good morning."

The man laughed. "It isn't morning; it's afternoon."

"Good afternoon," Izzy said.

"How are you this afternoon?"

"Okay," Izzy said. "How are you?"

"I'm okay, too. How come you're all by yourself? I bet you have lots of friends."

"Well, I have some."

"Do you have any brothers or sisters?"

"A brother, just one brother."

"What's his name?"

"Mike. My name's Izzy. What's your name?"

"Mr. Smith. Mike's your big brother?"

Izzy nodded.

"I bet he has lots of friends, too."

Izzy nodded.

"Who's Mike's best friend?"

"Bud."

"Do Bud and Mike let you play with them sometimes?"

"Sometimes."

"Sunday morning is a nice time to play together, isn't it? Did you and Mike and Bud play together yesterday morning?"

"Yesterday morning?" Izzy said.

"It's a lot of fun, isn't it, to play in the building project?"

"Building project?" Izzy said.

"Across Third on Ninety-fourth. Where they're tearing down all the houses. It's fun to play there, isn't it? You and Mike and Bud were playing there yesterday morning, weren't you?"

"No!" Izzy said. "We're not allowed!"

"Where does Bud live?"

"We don't play in the project!" Izzy said. "We're not allowed!"

"I'm not going to tell on you, Izzy; don't worry."

Mike came out of the house, and from the top of the stoop he saw his sister talking to the man. At first he was afraid it was the man in the car who had yelled at them yesterday when they came out of the project. Then he saw that it wasn't the same man, but there was something about him that scared Mike. He was one of those guys who are against kids, out to get them, some kind of cop. What was he talking to Izzy about anyway?

Mike heard him say to her, "Does Bud live in this block, too?"

"Hi," Mike said quickly, so that Izzy couldn't answer. He ran down the steps and sat between Izzy and the man. "What are you talkin' about?"

"We were just saying hello to each other," the man said, and grinned at him. "You must be Mike. Hi, Mike."

"I heard you ask her where Bud lives," Mike said.

"And," Izzy said, "he says we play there where they're tearin' all those houses down."

Oh, man, Mike thought, this one was from the building project. That guy in the car must have sent him to find the three of them. That's why he wanted to know where Bud lived, so he could pull all of them in together. He sure was out to get them.

"We don't play there," Mike said. "You can't even get in there."

"Oh, I bet there's a way," the man said, and winked at him. "And you look smart enough to find it."

"No," Mike said, "they got it all boarded up, all locked up. So kids can't get in."

"Forget about it," the man said. "Who cares? What's your favorite game, Mike? Stickball, basketball?"

"I don't care," Mike said.

"Don't you want to grow up to be another Willie Mays or another Wilt Chamberlain?"

"I don't care," Mike said. "I don't even want to grow up."

"You got to," the man said; "you can't help yourself. Izzy tells me that Bud is your best friend. Does he live in this block?"

"No," Mike said.

"Near here?"

"Not far away," Mike said. "We go to the same school."

"Where does he live?"

"Over across Second Avenue somewheres," Mike said. "Over there somewhere. I only see him in school."

Then he looked up and saw Bud coming down the street. He was almost to them. Mike chewed at his lip and tried to think what to do. Bud would stop and talk to them and the nosy guy would find out who he was. Or dumb little Izzy would say hello, Bud, and it was going to be bad.

Bud was right in front of them now, but to Mike's surprise he didn't stop or talk or anything. He was walking right past them, just like he didn't know them, just like he'd never seen them before, and didn't see them now.

Mike heard the scrape of feet behind them and he turned around. There was his mother standing on the top of the stoop. He saw her face get all stiff and mad as she saw Bud going by. That's why Bud didn't look at them or anything; Bud was smart.

"Hello, Mom!" Mike said.

"Hi, Mom!" Izzy said. "Is it suppertime yet? We're starvin'!"

She jumped up and ran up the stairs to her mother. Mike followed her. He didn't look back at the man.

"Yeah, Mom," he said, "we're starvin'! What's to eat?"

Mrs. Fernandez laughed and said, "It ain't near suppertime. But come on, I'll find you something so you don't starve!"

None of the kids hanging around the corner of Third and Ninety-fourth had seen Red the Cop since school. Bud had hurried around that block and two more without finding him. Out of breath, growing worried, he swung into his own block. Mike and Izzy were sitting on the stoop in front of his house, talking to some man. He didn't like the looks of the man, not a bit, he was another one of those inspectors or a company cop or something like that. He thought maybe he'd better call to Izzy and Mike and tell them to come along with him or something, but just then Mrs. Fernandez came out on the stoop. So he just walked right on by without even looking at them.

He kept right on walking, looking straight ahead. Then he saw Red the Cop down at the end of the block, and he forgot all about Izzy and Mike and the man. It was more important that he talk to Red, nothing was more important than that. Man, was he glad to see him. He crossed the street and broke into a run. Red would go with him to the cellar. Red would get help and he would have the man and the lady out of there in no time. He might even arrest the men that were trying to kill them if they were still hanging around. Bud would like to be there to see that. He saw Red get out his pad to write a ticket for a car that was parked too close to the corner. He wasn't more than ten yards from Red when he heard the voice behind him.

"Hey, Bud!"

It was his father. He pretended not to have heard him; he ran faster.

"Hey, Bud!"

It was no use. Everyone on the whole block heard him. Mr. Salter, who lived in the next house, stepped in front of Bud and said, "Your father wants you!"

Bud turned around and walked back to meet his father. He was laughing at Bud. "Where were you going in such a hurry? You got a girl?"

"No."

"You forget what day's today?"

"Yeah."

"But now you remember, huh?"

"Yeah."

Now he remembered, all right. It was Monday, his father's day off, and they all went to his grandparents in Queens for dinner every Monday. Bud tried to think of how he could get out of going.

"Look," he said, "you go without me, you and Mom."

"What's wrong?"

"I'm not feelin' so good. I'm sick kind of."

His father chuckled. "Is that where you were going in such a rush? To a doctor? Or maybe to the hospital?"

"No, it's nothin' serious," Bud said. "You and Mom don't have to stay home on account of me. I'll be all right alone. I'm not that sick. Besides, I got a whole lot of homework to do."

Now his father guffawed. "If you got a lot of homework that you're going to do, really do, Buddy-pal, then you are sicker than you know. You need an operation!"

Bud tried to smile. "Yeah, that's a good one. I need an operation. Look, you and Mom, you go. I have to run over to Jimmy Riorden's to borrow a book. I'm late. Say hello to Grandma and Grandpa for me."

Bud started off.

His father reached out and grabbed him by the shoulder. "Take it easy, son," he said. He wasn't smiling or laughing anymore. "What is all this bull?"

"What bull? There isn't any bull, honest!"

"What's going on?" His father's hand tightened on his shoulder and hurt him. He knew his father was beginning to get mad. "You up to something with those jig friends of yours?"

"No!"

"That Mike and Izzy from upstairs?"

"No! I don't play with them anymore!"

"Where you headed for just now? To play basketball with some of your other jig friends?"

"No! I don't have no other jig friends!"

"By God, you're going to tell me! What the hell is going on with you? Playing sick, got homework to do! You in some kind of trouble?"

"All right, I'll tell you!"

"You're damned right you'll tell me!"

"You're hurtin' my shoulder!"

"You're damned right I'm hurting your shoulder!"

Bud took a deep breath. "It's just that I don't want to go see Grandma and Grandpa!"

His father's hand dropped from his shoulder. "You don't want to go see your grandma and grandpa?"

"It's no fun out there, Pop! No television, nothin'! I just sit there and listen to you all talk."

"You never seemed to mind it, Bud. I thought you was having fun."

"I was just pretendin'! To be polite. But don't make me go, Pop, please! Not every single week! I'll go next week, honest!"

"You're damned right you'll go next week, and this week, and every week!" His father was getting mad again. "You was pretending, to be polite! Who the hell you think you are, pretending, just to be polite! You come the hell home with me and get the hell cleaned up and come the hell out to Queens with us! You can do some of all that homework you got to do out there after dinner."

His father swung him roughly around, marched him toward their house. Bud looked over his shoulder and saw Red the Cop tuck the parking ticket under the car's windshield wiper. Bud tried to think what to do now, but he couldn't even think anymore. He had done more thinking in this one day then he had all the rest of his life. And besides, he was scared. His father had almost found out about him and Mike and Izzy.

CHAPTER 14

"NINE," Larry said.

"Nine," Midge said. "Roger. Over."

Larry stood beneath the window, holding his watch up to the dirty, alley-cat-gray light. He was keeping Midge posted on the minutes as they passed since Bud had left them to go get Red the Cop. She had told him that it was not true that at times like these each minute seemed an endless hour. It varied. This minute could seem an endless hour and a quarter, that one an endless hour and three quarters. One of the minutes, just before she had asked him to keep her informed about them, had seemed, she said, well over two endless hours. She sincerely thought, she told him, that it would actually never end.

"Ten," Larry said.

"Ten," Midge said. "By now I would have thought it was at least a day and a half. Say! My spirits are rising, aren't they? How about yours, have they risen?"

"Need you ask? I never knew spirits could rise so high so fast."

"I love Bud," she said. "I love Red the Cop. Why, we'll be out of here in plenty of time for me to check in at the theater."

"Sure. And tonight Tony James will be sick. You'll go on for her and you'll be a sensation."

"It would happen on a Monday night," she said. "With the theater only half full. Monday night! It is Monday night, isn't it? My God, I have a date tonight with my crazy cousin! I promised to take her to the show! If I'm not at the theater to meet her, that nut will . . ." She stopped and peered at him in the half-light. "What is it? What's the matter, Larry?"

He stood looking at her, not able to speak. Her crazy cousin, she had said, and those words hit him like an electric shock. They tore away the curtain that had fallen on a part of his mind. The thing that he had been groping for now lay there before him, the locked-up memories came storming to the surface. Midge's crazy cousin had done it for him. Enid, too, had had a crazy cousin. . . .

The day he was remembering was coming back to him with a startling clarity. It was not long after he had come to the Costa Brava, soon after he had met Enid and Gerald. It was before Tom Bates had popped up unannounced for his stolen holiday.

The afternoon was blazing hot; it made a siesta necessary for one and all, native and outlander. The village of Cala Brava had awakened unwillingly, yawning and stretching. The iron shutters on the shop windows were reluctantly cranked open and merchandise unenthusiastically pushed out onto the sidewalks to trap the passing tourist trade. It was an afternoon that invited lethargy, complete torpor, but Enid had ignored the invitation. She was, as usual, abubble with energy, agog with enthusiasm. Inspiration had come her way, she said; she had had the most amusing idea.

"My cousin," Enid said. "That crazy, crazy cousin of mine! Gerald, Larry, you simply must meet her! And immediately!"

They were sitting in the shade of an ancient and retired corktree at a fishermen's café in the village's old plaza. Before them on the rickety wooden table were tiny platters of *tapas* and a sweating pitcher of iced *sangria*. Enid refilled their glasses with the sweet-tart fruit drink and lifted hers in a toast.

"To my darling crazy cousin!" she cried. Her high, clear British voice invaded every table in the square, penetrated all the surrounding shops. "My dears, you'll simply adore her! We must find her at once."

"Where," Gerald asked, "does one go looking for this demented relative of yours?"

"I hear that she has taken a villa for the summer somewhere near Cannes. I don't know exactly where. Neither, of course, does she."

"Cannes," Gerald said, and groaned. "All the way to Cannes in this weather? Enid, my dear. Enid, my darling of darlings . . ."

"Unbend, darling," Enid said. "Don't be so formal. Try a trifle harder."

"Light of my life," Gerald said with mock adoration. "My reason for being . . ."

"That loses a little in translation," Enid said, "but I'll accept it. What's on your mind?"

"This crazy cousin of yours," Gerald said. "Is she sufficiently mad to justify this trip? Larry and I won't be disappointed in her?"

"She is utterly, utterly mad," Enid said.

"That sounds mad enough," Larry said. "Mad enough for me."

"Thank you, darling," Enid said.

"Now, wait," Gerald said. "She isn't unattractive, is she? I mean she doesn't drool or scratch herself?"

"That is her charm," Enid said. "And I'm not saying this just because she is my cousin. She is utterly mad but she does not drool or scratch herself."

"How does she spend her time?" Larry asked.

"Disgracing her family," Enid said. "She's devoted to it. She spends hours on end at it."

"How exactly?" Gerald asked.

"Nudity, mainly," Enid said.

"That sounds rather mild," Gerald said, "in this day and age."

"Ah, but she cashes bad checks while in the nude! She trespasses, poaches, shoplifts, picks pockets, breaks and enters, she even does a bit of grave robbing while in the nude."

"What are her politics?" Gerald asked. "Sounds like a Communist to me."

"Oh, no!" Enid said. "She's a staunch Conservative, always has been."

"Very well," Gerald said. "I'll go."

They were on the road within the hour. They drove all night, spelling each other at the steering wheel and at a bottle of cognac, through Perpignan, Marseille, Toulon. They did not see Brigette Bardot in St. Tropez, but they saw dozens of girls who could have been her sister, and Gerald and Larry settled for that. After a late breakfast in Cannes they conscientiously bent to their task, the locating of Enid's crazy cousin.

They scoured the hill towns unsuccessfully, then when evening came they returned to the sea and went on to a small village only a few kilometers from Cannes. The little hotel that they checked into was frivolously built into the face of a cliff that hung over a narrow, rocky stretch of beach. Each of them, proclaiming publicly that they were bored with one another, went their separate ways. Enid had a letter to write, Gerald some pub-crawling to do, Larry a nap to take.

He had been dozing in his room for about twenty minutes when the phone rang. It was Enid. Her voice, always synthetically pitched in the key most people use to announce a fire, sounded almost hysterically gay.

"Larry!" she said. "Larry, darling, I have a surprise for you!"

"Your crazy cousin?"

"Yes, but guess what? Do try to guess!"

"You've located her, of course."

"Of course! But more than that. She's with me now! And I know you are longing to see her."

"I'll be right up."

"Room 905. And do hurry, darling."

He pushed his feet into moccasins, slipped into his jacket and ran up the three flights to room 905. His knuckles were still tapping at the door when it opened and Enid's voice lilted out into the hall.

"Darling, you did come quickly, didn't you? Do come in!"

He stepped into the small foyer. Enid closed the door, then sank back against it, her eyes closed. Through the glowing coat of tan Larry could see the sickly white pallor of her face. A shudder swept through her, convulsed her. Then she took a deep breath and opened her eyes. When she spoke, her voice was a whisper.

"It was rather awful, Larry."

"Where is she?"

Enid nodded toward the bedroom. From the doorway he could see the body of the woman that was sprawled across the foot of the bed. The blow on the temple that had killed her had broken the skin; the trickle of blood that ran down her cheek was making a tiny red pool in the curve of her throat. She had been an attractive woman, probably still in her early thirties. He heard Enid moving behind him; then she was standing at his side, looking silently down at the dead woman.

"You didn't find her here," he said.

She shook her head. "No, she found me. She came up here looking for me. I killed her."

In torment, in frustration, he pressed his fists against his temples. Through the darkness Midge stared at him, appalled and confused by what he had told her. She said nothing; there was no question she could think to ask. She could feel his fierce concentration as he tried to find some explanation for what had happened that day in the little village outside of Cannes.

"But it did happen!" His intensity exploded the silence. "It isn't an hallucination! It happened! I can see that room, Enid's face, the dead girl on the foot of the bed. I can hear Enid saying that she killed her."

"And then, Larry," Midge said softly. "After that, what happened?"

"And then . . . yes, then what happened . . ."

His voice dwindled off and she waited, breathlessly still, while he struggled to remember. At last he shook his head, defeated, and his sigh was a groan of despair.

"No, then there's nothing. After that I draw a complete blank."

"No police? No investigation?"

"Not that I remember."

"The dead girl . . . You don't know who she was?"

"I must have known then, Enid must have told me. But now . . ." He shook his head. "I don't know."

"Enid's cousin?"

"Yes . . . no, I don't know. She told me on the phone her cousin was with her. Maybe it was her cousin, but . . . oh, God, I can't remember anything!"

"You went back to Spain, Larry? Do you remember going back?"

"Yes, I remember driving back."

"You left right away? Right after the girl was killed?"

He was quiet for a long time. "No," he said at last, "we stayed the night at the hotel, I think. It was late in the afternoon when we left, almost dark. I think it must have been the next afternoon. I'm not sure."

"But you do remember the drive?"

"Some of it. We were drunk most of the time. I remember we picked up some beatnik somewhere and he drove for us, across the border."

"But you and Enid and Gerald didn't talk about it at all? Larry, there must have been something! Enid must have told you something!"

"Yes," he said, "you'd think so, wouldn't you? But if we talked about it, I don't remember what we said. It seems to me as though it couldn't ever have happened. But it did!

It *did* happen! Yes, wait . . . the next day . . . the next day . . ."

He stopped and she softly urged him on. "What was it, Larry? Something happened the next day. . . . What was it?"

"Everyone in the hotel was talking about it the next morning. During the night a girl had committed suicide. The desk clerk told us first; he was in a sweat about it. They thought the girl might have jumped from one of the hotel's windows. Her body was found on the rocks on the beach. . . ."

There was a furious, thundering roar. The walls of the house shook, the floor trembled beneath them, a stifling dust assailed them. Terrified, Midge flung herself into Larry's arms. His first thought was of the big bomb. Then it happened again, the thunderclap, followed by the cascading roar. Not the bomb, he thought. There was no need for two of the bomb. One would do. An earthquake, at least an earthquake. Thank God, he thought, it's only an earthquake.

It happened again, and again, and again, developing into a maniacal, murderous rhythm, and Larry realized that it was something as bad for them as the bomb and worse than an earthquake. The men who were to have rescued them had at last come back to work, and what they were doing would destroy them. One of those giant cranes with a swinging iron ball was knocking down the remaining walls of the gutted houses.

The clamorous noise, the violent tremors went on and on, came closer and closer. The cloud of dust thickened. Now, he thought, the hideous iron ball must be assaulting the very next house, and to prove that terrifying thought, a fall of debris blocked their window completely and plunged them into absolute blackness. He tightened his arms around Midge and held her closer to him, but he could find no words of hope or comfort to whisper into her ear, and he damned himself again for bringing her with him into what was to be a deathtrap.

Outside, not far away, he heard a piercing whistle blow. There was one more devastating blast against the house next door that made their walls shudder and fight against collapse. The quitting signal must have caught the ball in full swing. Then there was silence, and the thought came to him that now nobody would find them, not even the people who meant to murder them. They could shout their lungs out but, with the one window buried, no one could possibly hear them. They were completely entombed. And tomorrow this house would be struck down, and that would be it for them.

Then as the thick dust began to settle, he saw a glimmer of light that was seeping through the top of one of the side walls. He crawled through the newly fallen rubble and saw that the death-dealing iron ball might have turned into a life-saving instrument. He smoothed his hand over the wall; a loosened brick came out in his hand. He pried unsuccessfully at another. Groping around in the darkness, he found a piece of two-by-four. He patted it gratefully. With its help he might be able to knock out enough of a hole to crawl through into the next cellar, and from that cellar there might be some escape.

He was able now to say a word of hope to Midge. She was glad to hear it, almost hysterically glad. He set to work. It wasn't going to be easy, it would probably take a long time, but then, they both agreed, it was well worth the effort.

CHAPTER 15

MRS. FERNANDEZ was tired. She had left for work before Mike and Izzy went to school. On Mondays she cleaned for the Weavers who had a big, old-fashioned apartment all the way down in Greenwich Village and it was a lot of work and a long trip besides. Then there was still her own housework to be done. She had finished doing the kitchen, now she must do the children's room. On the way to their bedroom she flopped down in a chair in the living room and watched a TV movie for a few minutes with the kids. Then she sighed, pulled herself together, got out of the chair and went into the bedroom. She couldn't have been more surprised. She laughed out loud and clapped her hands.

"Isabelita!" she called out in delight. "Miguel!"

"Yes, Mama?" Miguel called back.

She stepped back into the living room. "You are a good boy, Miguel, and Isabelita, you are a good girl. You made your own beds! Or did you make Isabelita's, too, Miguel?"

"No!" Isabelita said. "I made mine all by myself!"

"You are not only a good girl," her mother said, "you are a big girl, too, now!"

"I'm gonna make my own bed every day," Isabelita said.

"How lucky I am to have two such nice children!" Mrs. Fernandez said. She went back into the bedroom. "Let me see what a good job you did."

"No!" Isabelita cried. "Don't look at mine!"

She jumped to her feet and ran after her mother, but she stopped in the doorway. Mrs Fernandez had already pulled back the bedspread and, puzzled, she turned to look at Isabelita. Miguel was standing beside her now and they were both staring at her with wide, frightened eyes.

"Why, Isabelita," her mother said, "where is your blanket?"

Isabelita shook her head and began to sniffle.

Mrs. Fernandez' voice rose sternly. "Isabelita, why are you crying? Have you done something bad? What did you do with your blanket? Answer me!"

Isabelita's sniffle burst into a torrent of tears. She ran to the sofa in the living room, threw herself face down upon it, the tears turning into a wail.

Mrs. Fernandez, frowning, turned to Miguel. "Miguel," she said, "what is the matter? You tell me."

"I don't know, Mama."

"Yes, you know; yes, you do! I can see it in your face!"

"No, Mama! Maybe somebody stole the blanket or . . ."

"You are telling a lie to me!" She took Miguel by the shoulders and shook him angrily. "What did you do with the blanket?"

"Nothing, Mama!"

"You are afraid to tell me, Miguel. Why are you afraid? Miguel, you are a good boy, I know you have done nothing wrong. . . ." She stopped and said sharply, "It is only when you play with that whitey friend of yours downstairs that there is trouble. Is that it? Is that why you and Isabelita are frightened? Did you give the blanket to Bud?"

"No, Mama!"

"Yes! You are playing with him again. He is making you do something wrong. He is getting you in trouble. Why did you give him the blanket?"

"No, Mama, we didn't. . . ."

"I am going to find out, Miguel! Come along, and you, too, Isabelita. We will go downstairs this minute! We will find out about this!"

"They aren't home, Mama! Today they go to his grandmother's house, every Monday!"

"Then we will wait until they come home! I will find out what Bud has got you into this time! That Bud, he brings nothing but trouble!"

The night watchman was sorely troubled; last night he had grievously jeopardized his job. He had fallen asleep on duty. This had shaken him; it had never happened before. He could not understand it. That is, he pretended to himself that he couldn't understand it. He was afraid that he knew the answer only too well. He was getting too old for the job. Nine years ago, when he had started to work for the demolition company, he had lied about his age. Actually, he had been seventy-two, not sixty-five. Actually, he was now eighty-one, not seventy-four. But his wife said, had said, in fact, just the other day, that he didn't look a day over seventy-four.

He agreed with her. He didn't feel a day over seventy-four and, if he said so himself, his wife was right about him not looking it. He wasn't ready for the scrap heap yet. But last night he had fallen asleep on duty. Not nodded, not dozed. From just before ten until well after four he had slept soundly, like the proverbial log. For the life of him he could not explain it. He had slept well the day before, his usual six hours. In the late afternoon he had gone to a movie with Martha, as they did several times a week, then they had taken their customary stroll in Prospect Park. At seven-thirty he had eaten his usual light supper. He couldn't blame his falling asleep on overfatigue or overeating. At nine-thirty, in the plywood hut, he had boiled water on the electric grill for coffee, instant coffee. The usual strength. He had drunk it down, and the next thing he knew it was four o'clock in the morning.

Well, he would make sure that it didn't happen again. As the water on the electric hot plate came to a boil, he took up the jar of Nescafe and spooned double his usual amount into the cup, double his usual strength. Not only would he stay awake all night, he thought, and smiled at the exaggeration of his thought, he probably wouldn't sleep a wink all day tomorrow.

The coffee was too strong for his taste, but he drank it all down. Then settling into his chair to smoke a quiet pipe before starting on his first rounds, he faced the night with confidence. Ten minutes later he was dead to the world.

The man used his flashlight briefly to assess how much the crane operator had been able to accomplish in the short time he had worked that afternoon. He saw that the crane had wreaked a surprising amount of devastation. Another wall had bit the dust, and the top floor of another building. He switched off his flash, thinking that if Jacoby and the girl had been hiding hereabouts there was no need to continue the search. They would have been buried alive; one day a bulldozer would disinter what was left of them.

He moved on past the next house and came to a sudden stop. From somewhere nearby came the faint, muted sound of an almost rhythmic tapping. It seemed to be coming from the cellar of the house that he had just passed. He quietly investigated, and discovered that there was no way to get into that house or its cellar. Debris blocked the door and the cellar and the first-floor windows. The entrance to the house beside it, still fairly intact, was clear. He made his way into the rear room of the ground floor and stood there, listening. The tap-tap-tap now seemed to be directly below him. He crept down the stairs to the cellar, cautiously, not making a sound, not even risking the use of his light.

At the foot of the stairs he stopped. There was no doubt about it at all now; the tapping was coming from the other side of the cellar wall. He smiled in the darkness.

It had to be Jacoby. He pulled his gun from its shoulder holster and sat down on the steps to wait for Jacoby to get on with his job. Keep at it, Jacoby, he thought; keep at it, boy; you're doing fine.

"Mark my words," Bud's grandfather said to his father, "Ike will go down in history as one of the best Presidents we ever had."

"And don't underestimate Truman," his father said.

"And just imagine," his mother said to his grandmother, "only a dollar-ninety a yard."

"How many yards did you get?" his grandmother asked.

"Buddy," his grandfather said, and squeezed his knee, "who do you think was the best President?"

"I don't know," Bud said. "George Washington, I guess."

He tried to not think about the man and the lady; it made him feel sort of sick. He kept telling himself that somehow they got out of there, they were okay now, safe and sound. He kept telling himself that.

"What I thought I'd do," his mother said, "is put the living room ones in our bedroom."

"He's been a good governor," his grandfather said, "an outstanding governor, and he'll make a good president."

"He's got my vote," his father said, and stood up. "Well, honey, what do you say we head for home?"

"Yes," his mother said, "it's time Bud got to bed."

"Say, Bud," his grandfather said, "I'm going fishing tomorrow out at Montauk Point. How would you like to stay here overnight and go with me?"

"Shame on you for suggesting that," his mother said. "Tomorrow's a school day."

"Missing one day of school," his grandfather said, "won't hurt him. How about it, Bud?"

"Thanks," Bud said, "but I ought to go home and go to school tomorrow."

His father laughed and said, "I must be going deaf. I thought I heard Bud say he ought to go to school tomorrow."

"No, Bud didn't say that," his grandfather said. "He said he's going fishing with me. Didn't you, Bud?"

"No," Bud said, "I got to go to school, but thanks."

"He said it again!" his father said. "Is that kid standing there my kid, Bud Brady?"

"He's been acting kind of funny all day," his mother said.

"You can say that again!" his father said. "We better get him to bed. Good night, folks."

He had no idea how long he had been working on the wall. He suggested to Midge, and she readily agreed, that she give him a watch with a luminous dial for Christmas. The hole's growth was excruciatingly slow. Each brick took on a nasty, stubborn character of its own. He used the two-by-four as sparingly as possible, making as little sound as possible. He would tap at a brick just enough to jar it slightly loose, then finish the job with his bare hands. All of his fingernails were broken, his knuckles, without exception, were raw and bleeding. But he persevered, not minding, at the moment, this type of work at all. It could prove rewarding. As the empty space in the wall widened and lengthened, a beautiful grayness appeared behind it, suggesting that there was some kind of opening in the cellar beyond, an opening that would be their escape hatch.

Twice he stopped to test the hole for size; the first time it proved impossibly tight across the shoulders; the second time he could almost press through it. Then, with success so near, he began to work feverishly and at last it was big enough for him to squirm through, a cinch for Midge.

"We've got it made, Midge," he told her. "I'm going through."

"And I," she said, her voice chipper, "will not be far behind."

He snaked through the opening headfirst. On the other side his hands hit the concrete of the floor; he turned a slovenly somersault and scrambled to his feet. As he turned back to extend a helping hand and a word of encouragement to Midge, a beam of light hit him on the chest. He raised an arm to shield his eyes against the glare and he could make out the blurred silhouette of a man. The man took a step toward him and now Larry could see the hand that held the flashlight and the other one holding a gun that was leveled at him.

Then, suddenly, the figure of the man was engulfed. With a weary groan the ceiling above him collapsed. Larry heard him cry out in shock and pain. The flashlight, still lit, came spinning across the room, and Larry snatched it up and swung its beam to where he had last seen the man with the gun. He was half buried in a mass of debris. A beam had fallen across his chest; from ankles to shoulders he was covered with rubbish. His gun hand was immobilized, twisted beneath him. Larry could see the muzzle of the gun protruding from beneath the man's back.

He wheeled around to flash the light on the wall behind him.

"Midge!" he shouted.

He saw that the hole he had come through was gone, an avalanche of bricks and mortar had filled and blocked it.

"Midge!" he shouted again.

Her voice came faintly to him. "Larry . . . Larry, are you all right?"

"I'm all right. Midge . . ."

"Can you get out? Is there a way out? . . ."

He swung the light in an arc around him and saw what he had been afraid he would see—the stairway had been blocked by the cave-in, and there was nothing he could do about it without help. The obstructing beams were too heavy for one person to lift. He looked for some other opening that he might clear; there was none. He had painfully worked his way from one inescapable prison to another, separating him and Midge. The thought of telling her made him sick.

The half-buried man groaned and said something, but he heard Midge's voice through the wall. Her words were indistinguishable.

"Midge, I can't hear you. . . . Can you hear me?"

"Yes . . ."

"There's no way out here. . . ."

"Larry, listen to me!" With his ear pressed against the wall, he could just make out her words. "I said I can get out! There's a hole right above me. I can get out easy. Do you understand?"

"Yes . . ."

"I can get out, Larry! I'll get help. I'll get the police!"

"Midge!" He decided he wouldn't tell her about the man with the gun. "Midge, be careful! Remember they're still out there. . . ."

"I'll be careful, Larry. . . ."

Cautiously, testing every step before she made it, Midge inched her way up the slope of rubble toward the narrow, jagged opening that the cave-in had created. When she reached it, she stopped, listening for a moment, then she warily lifted her head through it and looked about her. In the night light the place looked like a block that had been bombed, full of gaping craters and ugly mountains of waste. She wriggled through the opening and stopped again to look and listen. There was no movement and no sound except the rumble of the outside traffic. She used an instant, but only an instant, to take one breath of the lovely, freshly polluted air before she forced herself to move out into the open.

She was sure that the house they had come through to get inside the project was on the opposite side of the block; she was fairly certain that it was almost directly across from where she was now standing. Using the stacks of lumber, the piles of brick, the pieces of machinery as cover, she threaded a path across the project. Several times, when she heard a sound or saw a shadow that might be a threat to her, she froze in her tracks, but she finally made it. She had crossed her no-man's land. The first house she went into was not the right one; its street door was sealed, its windows boarded. In the second she found the door with the removable panel.

Now she was standing in the vestibule, and she discovered that she was trembling. Her next move would be the most dangerous one. There would be men, she knew, on every street surrounding the site, watching for them, waiting for them. Somehow she must find a way to get down off that stoop and out of that block without being seen.

She flattened herself against the vestibule wall, dared to peek out into the street. It looked ordinary, harmless; there were cars parked bumper to bumper along the curbs, street lights shining down upon them. A group of teen-agers straggled past, a couple strolling a dog, a woman steering home a drunken man. Two or three cars rolled by, an occupied taxi, and then she thought, why, of course! It would be a simple matter getting out of here. She would call a cab. It wouldn't matter if they did see her coming out of the house. She would be in the cab, off and away, before they could catch her.

She remembered a conversation she had had with Larry. The more you needed a cab, they agreed, the less chance of getting one. But she had boasted that she was lucky that way. Be lucky now, she prayed. Lady Luck, please send an empty cab down this street, and soon. The prayer was answered, though not immediately. It seemed forever she had been standing pressed against that wall before a taxi with a liberty light glowing on its roof came down the street. When it was just abreast of her, she darted out onto the stoop, put two fingers to her lips and whistled as she had never whistled before, whistled as though her life, and Larry's, depended upon it. One whistle was enough; she saw the cab jerk to a stop, as though all four of its wheels had simultaneously fallen off. She raced down the steps, squeezed between two parked cars and lunged into the cab.

"Where to, miss?"

"To the police, to the nearest policeman!"

"What?"

"Go, go, go!" she pleaded. "Get out of here!"

The cabbie, with no further questions, shoved the car in gear and stepped on the gas. Midge did not see the car parked at the corner behind her pull away from the curb. She did see the car, a black sedan, back away from the curb ahead of them. It stopped in the middle of the street, blocking their way. The taxi driver jammed on his brakes and the cab stopped so suddenly that the car coming at them from behind crashed into their rear. Midge was thrown forward. She felt, a sharp, hot pain as her forehead hit the back of the front seat. Then she felt nothing at all.

A moment later when the cabbie was able to climb out of his taxi, the driver of the car ahead was there to meet him. He hit him once on the chin and, as he fell, once on the back of the neck. The cabbie crumpled onto the street. The driver of the car behind joined the other driver. Together they lifted Midge out of the cab and carried her to the first car. It then drove off.

CHAPTER 16

THE MAN TRAPPED by the beam and the debris moaned and pleaded again with Larry to free him. He had said that he was the night watchman and for a moment Larry had believed him, had wanted to believe him. He had seen in the glow of the flashlight that he had the face of a respectable workingman. He could have heard the sound of digging and come to investigate—with a gun in one hand, naturally, and a flashlight in the other. He could be the watchman.

It would take no more than a few minutes, Larry saw, to clear away the rubble that almost buried the man. With that done he could get at the heavy beam that was pinioning him to the cellar floor. At his feet lay a ten-foot length of two-by-four; he could use it as a lever to pry up the beam and free him. Together, if the man was not too badly injured, they could quite possibly clear the stairs and make their escape. They would not have to wait for Midge to come back with the police; they could be out of here in a matter of minutes.

But there would be that one moment when he lifted the beam and the man's body would be free that he could not risk. For in that moment the hand that was twisted beneath him, the gun still clenched in it, would also be free. Before Larry could throw himself at the man, wrench the gun from him, he would have time to fire it point-blank at him. He knew that he couldn't risk it. If the man wasn't shamming, if his groans of pain were real, he would have to suffer a little while longer. Sorry, old boy, he thought; but that's the way it has to be.

It needn't be much longer. Midge had been gone almost ten minutes. By now she might be out of this damned place, already telling her story to the police. It might take another ten minutes for them to get here, and then it would be all over. Or at least, it would be the beginning of the end. He would find Vic Jacoby; he would know what to do about the boys who were trying so earnestly to kill him.

He was thinking about Vic Jacoby, how in God's name he would go about finding him when suddenly, unbidden and unheralded, another part of his forgotten past flashed across his mind. . . .

He was back in the small room in the hotel on the French Riviera; he could feel the heat of the late afternoon sun streaming through the window, hear the surf beating on the rocks below. He could see Enid's face, white and strained, and the twisted, lifeless face of the girl sprawled on the bed.

Enid seemed to have shaken herself out of her shock. Her face had become expressionless, her voice low and grim.

"I hadn't any choice," she said. "She came after me. I realized it just in time."

"Yes," he said. "What about Gerald? Does he know?"

She shook her head. "I tried to ring him after I talked to you. He isn't in his room. Larry . . . what do we do now?"

"We can't do anything until dark. You'll make sure that no one gets in here, finds her."

"Yes."

"I'll round up Gerald. We'll arrange something." He opened the door a sliver and saw that the hall was empty. He turned back to Enid. "You'll be all right?"

"Yes," she said. She had gone to the window, her back was to the still figure on the bed. "Yes, I'm all right."

The next morning everyone was talking about the tragedy, and everyone seemed to have a different theory about it. One group said it was obviously murder. Another said that it was obviously suicide. A third group, conservatives, preferred to think it an accident. It had to be one of the three; the young woman had certainly either been thrown or had jumped or fallen to her death. Her battered body had been found just after dawn on the rocks below the hotel. The police had questioned everyone, including Enid and Gerald and Larry, whose rooms all faced the sea, overlooking the rocks. No one, apparently, had seen or heard anything that might help the police. The police were unable to identify the body and if they had any theory about the woman's death, they kept it to themselves.

Just before noon Enid and Gerald and Larry had gone out on the crowded terrace for a drink. They were immediately besieged by a battalion of young people, old Riviera friends of Enid and Gerald. They were all beautiful creatures, all tall and slender with carefully tended sun tans. They had stopped by the hotel for a quick drink; they were on their way to a luncheon party in the hills. A fabulous villa, they said, built by a fabulous American couple. There was a great circular swimming pool and cool, shady terraces. There would be good food and endless champagne, and Enid and

Gerald and their friend Larry must absolutely join them.

Enid demurred. They had thought they might start back for Spain, she said; by leaving early they might avoid some of the weekend traffic. Her friends were aghast.

"Darling Enid," one of them said, "surely you didn't hear me? There will be champagne without end; it flows and flows and flows. This isn't like you, darling Enid. . . ."

Laughing, Enid and Gerald had agreed to go. Larry had other things to do, he said, some film to buy in Cannes, other errands to attend to. He would pick them up at the fabulous villa sometime in the late afternoon; from there they would go on to the Costa Brava. He waved them off, three cars full of them, and saw them disappear around a curve in the road leading up to the hills.

He drove his car out of the hotel garage and onto the road to Cannes. He had gone only a few blocks when the motor sputtered and came to a stop. He checked the gasoline; there was plenty. He tried again to start it, but the motor coughed and died. There was a garage at the corner and the mechanic amiably took over; he said that if in an hour he had not repaired the damage, he would at least know what was wrong.

It was high noon now. Away from the beach, where there was no sea-cooled breeze, the sun was blistering hot and Larry walked down a palm-lined side street to the water and stopped at a small café on the esplanade. The heat had driven more than even the usual hordes to the seashore; the sand was strewn with basking figures, the café terrace was almost filled. Still, he saw the two men who had been following him the moment they climbed the steps to the bar. He had noticed them first across the street from the garage where he had left the car to be repaired. He ordered a beer, then changed the order to a whiskey. The last twenty-four hours had been tough ones, the next few might prove equally tough.

"Excuse me," a voice said, "but are you not Larry Towers?"

The men were standing beside his table, smiling down at him. One was quite tall and thin, almost spindly, with an angular face and pale blue eyes. The other was tall, too, but heavy-set and dark-skinned, and he had a German camera slung over one shoulder.

"Yes," he said, "I'm Towers."

"I mean the Larry Towers," the thin one said. "The well-known writer and photographer."

"Well," he said. "I'm a writer and I'm a photographer."

"I thought I recognized you back there at the garage! I said so to my friend. Please, may we sit down with you for a minute or two?"

"Sure," Larry said.

"I am Adam Knapp," he said. He sat on the one chair, dragged another from the next table for his friend. "This is Carl Wicker, an old friend of mine. I am a great admirer of your work, Mr. Towers."

"Thanks."

"And it is very fortunate for me that I meet you. You see, I am also a writer of sorts. A reporter for a newspaper in a small town near Essen. So if you would grant me an interview it would be a great scoop for me. Isn't that true, Carl?" He nudged his friend's arm, but didn't wait for him to agree. "It won't take up much of your time. A few questions only, and perhaps you will permit Carl to take a picture of you and me together. My editor will be impressed."

"I'm afraid," Larry said, "that you are making a mistake. I am not all that well known. I just about make a living."

"You underrate yourself, Mr. Towers. Now you have been

earning your living this way for how long?"

"Quite awhile. Six or seven years."

"And before that?"

"I did photography for an advertising agency."

"Oh, yes, of course. On your West Coast, was it not?"

"No, in Chicago. That's the Midwest."

"But you came from the West Coast originally, is that not so?"

"Yes. I was born there. I went to school there."

"But you seem lately to have deserted your homeland."

"I go back occasionally."

"You seem mainly however to be doing your stories here. In France and Spain."

"Yes."

"Is there any special reason for that?"

"Well, the Riviera, the Costa Brava make good copy. Girls in bikinis make good copy."

"Are you here now on some certain story?"

"No. On a holiday."

"You are sure that the tragedy here had nothing to do with your visit? It might make rather a sensational story, might it not? Violence on the Riviera, that sort of thing?"

"No, that's not my type of thing. Happy holidays, that's my line."

"But what is your theory about it? Was it murder or suicide or an accident?"

"I have no theory."

It was then that he saw the girl coming down the esplanade toward them. She was obviously an American; she had that swinging stride, that way of carrying her shoulders and her head. She was wearing a jade-green bikini, the ultimate in bikinis, and in the sunlight her hair was a dazzling blonde.

She was barefoot. She was looking directly at him and smiling. He was sure that he knew her from someplace, but couldn't think where or when. But there was a sure though surprised recognition in her eyes and in a moment she would reach his table. Then it struck him who the girl was and he knew he had to move quickly.

"Excuse me," he said to the two men. "I seem to have forgotten a date for lunch."

He jumped up from the table, took three long steps and managed to intercept her at the terrace stairs, his hands outstretched. He saw her mouth opening to say his name and he spoke loud and quickly.

"Midge!" he said. "Well, hello, Midge!"

He turned her around and started her back up the esplanade.

"Those people I was with," he said, "are very dreary people, even if you like people." The strollers on the broad tiled walk were moving too slowly for him; he wanted to put more distance between him and the men he had left in the café. He stepped down onto the sand, then reached up and swung Midge down beside him. "Let's walk on the beach," he said.

"Sure," she said, and started trotting along beside him. "You didn't recognize me at first, did you, Vic?"

"No. What have you done to yourself?"

"Grown up, I suppose."

He laughed. "How time flies." Out of the corner of his eye he saw the man who called himself Adam Knapp signal the waiter.

"You haven't been in New York for a long time, have you?" she said. "At least, no one seems to have seen you. I keep asking around." She stopped. "Here, here," she said to a small boy who was destroying a small girl's sand castle. "None of that now!"

He took her by the hand and drew her along. "The last time I was in New York," he said, "about a year and a half ago, I asked around about you."

"Did you? Really?"

"I did. Somebody told me you were an actress. Very successful." They had reached a covy of refreshment stands on the beach side of the esplanade. Here, around them, it was crowded, a small Coney Island on the Fourth of July. He stopped in front of one of them and looked back, scanning the oncomers. He did not see either of the two men.

Midge was laughing. "Yes, I'm big in Pittsburgh. I've spent most of my time on the road, but I've got a job in New York lined up for this fall. I'm going to be stand-by for Tony James in a new play."

He said, "I'd rather see you in a play than Tony James."

"Would you? Really?" she asked delightedly. "Well, confidentially, I can act rings around Tony James."

"I bet you can. How long are you going to be here, Midge?" He looked up and saw that somehow the man called Carl had got ahead of them. He was standing on the edge of the esplanade, his eyes searching the crowd. He hadn't seen them yet, but in another moment it was inevitable that he should. He turned, but he knew that somewhere behind him the other man would be walking. He looked for an escape. There was the sea on one side, and he was not in bathing trunks. A café on the other side would offer a momentary haven.

He found a table beside a window that overlooked the beach; there was, he noted with satisfaction, a second door leading out onto the esplanade. Through the window he saw

Carl, still standing where he had seen him last; he glanced in the opposite direction; again he could not locate the one called Adam.

He looked at Midge, sipping a Compari, tanned face glowing, smiling as she told him about her new job.

"It's a featherbrained play, Vic, but Tony and Sandy are both good names. They'll keep it running for a while, anyway."

"What are your chances of playing the part? How healthy is Miss James?"

"She's strong as a horse."

"Maybe she'll break a leg and they'll have to shoot her."

Midge grinned. "I don't wish her a broken leg, but honestly, I won't mind if she sprains an ankle occasionally."

They drank their drinks and talked and he kept one eye on the beach. After a few minutes he saw Adam, tall enough to stand out above the people milling about him; he had joined the one called Carl and they were in conference. Then Adam turned and began walking back the way he had come; Carl turned and went the other way. This, Larry knew, was the time to move.

He looked at his watch and pretended surprise. "My God, it's after one. I'm sorry, Midge, but I promised some people I'd have lunch with them." He put some money on the table. "Where are you staying?"

"The Victor Hugo."

"I'll walk you there, if that's where you're going."

"Thanks, I am, Vic."

He was sure he was in the clear as they left the café and the beach and walked the short block to her hotel.

"I'll call you this afternoon," he said. "Can we have dinner tonight? Maybe do something afterwards?"

"Oh, fine! Let's go gambling."

"It's a deal," he said. "The casino at Cannes."

At the entrance to her hotel she said, "Tonight I'll be wearing a dress and shoes. Will you recognize me?"

He laughed and said, "From now on I'll know you anywhere, in anything. On the moon in a space suit. Try me."

"I'll do that, Vic."

They both laughed.

He headed back to the garage to see if his car was ready to roll. This phase of their mission, the one they called Operation Crazy Cousin, was finished. He would make the report to his superior, and he and Enid and Gerald would be given their next assignment.

The sight of the Brady family climbing the stoop, their white faces luminous in the street light, re-ignited Mrs. Fernandez' anger. Isabelita had cried herself to sleep on the sofa. Mrs. Fernandez had relented enough to carry her into her bed and to cover her with her own blanket. Miguel had remained awake, silent and sullen. Threats, slaps, cajolery, bribes, nothing had been able to make him speak, and this had frightened Mrs. Fernandez. The trouble that that Bud had got her Isabelita and Miguel into must be very, very bad. She turned away from the window.

"They are here," she said. "Come now."

Miguel slid out of his chair and darted toward the bedroom, but his mother was too quick for him. She grasped him by the back of his collar, forcing him to move ahead of her. As she opened the hall door, she heard the Bradys on the stairs below. She waited until their apartment door had opened and closed; she did not want the neighbors to hear what she had to say to those whiteys. With each step down the stairway her rage, fueled now by her fear, grew stronger. She pounded on the Bradys' door.

It was Bud who opened the door. The look on his face as Mrs. Fernandez shoved Miguel through the doorway proved to her without any doubt that he was at the bottom of this.

"What the hell!" Brady said, coming into the living room. He saw Mrs. Fernandez and her son and his voice rose to an angry shout. "What the hell is this?"

Then her maternal rage and the fury of her racial frustration overwhelmed Mrs. Fernandez. She was screaming at Bud's father, first in English, then in a mixture of English and Spanish, then entirely in Spanish. Brady was shouting back at her, shaking his fist in her face.

Mrs. Brady came running in from the kitchen, shocked by the din. At first she simply stood there, watching helplessly, wringing her hands. Suddenly Bud could stand it no longer. He charged his father, beating at him with his fists, kicking him in the shins. Brady fell back under the furious assault, and Bud drove him into a sitting position on the studio couch.

"She's Mike's mother!" Bud yelled. "Don't you talk to her like that!"

For a moment there was silence in the room. Bud's father blinked at him in astonishment and rubbed his shins. "My own kid," he said. "My own kid hit me; he socked me."

"Don't talk to her like that," Bud said fiercely. "She's Mike's mother."

Mrs. Brady said quietly, "Bud's right."

Mr. Brady gaped at his wife.

"You shouldn't talk to her like that," she said. "Not to anyone, no matter what color they are."

"Well, I'll be damned!" Brady said. "First my own kid,

then my own wife."

"Something's wrong," Mrs. Brady said. "Something to do with Bud and her children. Bud's been acting strange all day. Mrs. Fernandez, what did you come to tell us?"

Calmed by Mrs. Brady's tone, Mrs. Fernandez told them about the missing blanket. She told of Mike and Izzy's frenzied reaction when she had discovered it gone. She dropped her accusation that Bud was at the bottom of it all and completely to blame. Instead she said that she was sure the children had been playing together again, had done something they shouldn't have done, something bad, and somehow the blanket was involved.

"Bud," Mr. Brady roared, "if you been playing with them little . . ."

"Shut up," Mrs. Brady said. "Keep quiet. That's no way to handle this. Just look at Bud and Mike. They're scared to death."

"Yes," Mrs. Fernandez said. "And my Isabelita, she is scared to death, too."

"Bud," Mrs. Brady said, "what have you been doing?"

"Nothing."

"You and Izzy and Mike have been playing together, haven't you?"

"No."

Mrs. Brady looked helplessly at Mrs. Fernandez. Mrs. Fernandez said, "Miguel, you tell me."

"There's nothing to tell!"

"Bud," Mrs. Brady said suddenly, "have you been playing in the building project again? Is that it?"

"No!"

Mrs. Brady knew that he had answered too quickly, too loudly. "Listen, Bud," she said, "maybe you won't tell us because you're afraid what your father will do to you. But if I promise you he won't do anything, then will you tell?"

Bud considered. "Maybe if he promises, I'll tell."

Mrs. Brady looked at her husband.

"Okay," he said. "If you think this is the way to handle this, okay."

"You promise?" Bud said to him.

"I promise. For God's sake, yes, I promise!"

Bud turned to Mrs. Fernandez. "Will you promise about Mike and Izzy?"

"Yes," Mrs. Fernandez said. "I promise."

"Okay," Bud said, and took a deep breath. "Well, yeah, we been playin' in the buildin' project again. We were playin' there yesterday mornin' and we found this lady and man stuck down in a cellar. They couldn't get out and somebody, some gangsters, they said, were tryin' to kill them. . . ."

"To kill them!" his mother said.

"That's what they told me," Bud said. "And I took them things to eat and Izzy's blanket and mine to keep them warm. . . ."

His father slapped his thigh and snorted with laughter. "Brother, now I heard everything! Bud, this is something you seen on television!"

"I'll show you!" Bud cried. "C'mon, I'll take you where they are!"

CHAPTER 17

THE MAN who could possibly be the night watchman, or might be a killer with a gun, was quiet now. He had given up trying to talk Vic into releasing him. Occasionally Vic flicked the light across the man's face and now he saw hatred burning in his eyes. He couldn't honestly blame the man.

He turned the light onto his watch. Midge might be on her way back with the police by now. He found himself straining to hear the sound of sirens. Perhaps it was a little too soon to expect her, too quick, but his optimism did not falter. He had a strong, good feeling that she had got safely out of the block. She was clever, resourceful and tough . . . and he thought with a wry, grim smile, she knew Vic Jacoby when she saw him. She had recognized him at fifty yards that day on the Riviera, and that more recent evening in the bar on Times Square she had not been wrong in calling him Vic Jacoby. She had been right, and the enemy agents who were trying to kill him had been right. He was Vic Jacoby.

How had it happened that he had completely blacked out Vic Jacoby and become completely Larry Towers? It had happened during the tragedy in Spain and there, of course, lay the explanation. When an enemy bullet had sent his car hurtling off the road, as he had watched his three friends plunge to their horrible death, his mind had revolted. He had rejected the dangerous, often ugly life of Vic Jacoby, espionage agent, for the carefree happy life of Larry Towers, free-lance writer and photographer.

And, good God, how completely he had become Larry Towers! He had accepted as fact all the details of Larry Towers' life that had been so carefully invented, so meticulously organized to provide a cover for Vic Jacoby to hide behind. It had all become true to him! The childhood on the West Coast, the elderly aunt who had raised him after his parents died . . . He had thought that was his actual life. The schools and college in California, the job in Chicago—he had accepted it all. Vic Jacoby had disappeared from his mind as though he had never been. There was only Larry Towers.

Now the realities of Vic Jacoby's life began to come back to him. Some of them he would prefer not to remember, some were pleasant. Among the pleasant ones were the times he spent in New York between assignments, those days in the Village. He smiled now as he remembered the little blonde named Midge something, the tangle-haired, bright, pretty kid in blue jeans and sandals who was still in school somewhere. He used to see her on the street and in the coffee houses and she was always so enthusiastically glad to see him that it embarrassed him. She was so young.

More names and faces, more times and places came crowding back into his mind, not neatly, but in a torrential jumble. And now he began to understand what had been happening to him.

He had left Spain so suddenly that his fellow agents there, his contacts, had lost him. The enemy had lost him, too, but not for long. They had meant for him to die, of course, with the others in the crash. When he had escaped, they had followed him to New York. His behavior must have puzzled them. He had reported nothing of what he, as Vic Jacoby, had learned about the enemy in France and Spain to his superiors. In New York he had gone on living the life of Larry Towers, his own cover. To the enemy the only explanation would be that he was defecting, that he was ready to come over to them.

They had assigned Polly Grant to sound him out, and she had realized the truth. She knew that he was not a potential defector but a victim of amnesia. In that state he was no danger to them; he was harmless. But how long would that state continue? A day would certainly come when his memory would return, and they could not let that happen. The hunt was on again.

His attempt to prove to them that he was not Vic Jacoby had been futile. The only person he had convinced was Midge, and he had to smile when he realized why she had believed him. She had reluctantly conceded that he was not Vic Jacoby because Vic, she said, was taller. The night he had met her in the bar she had been wearing high spiked heels and she had come almost to his chin. Before that, the times in the Village and that one day on the Riviera, she had been in sandals or barefoot. Then she had just come to his shoulder.

Once again in the glow of the flashlight he looked at his watch, and his heart plummeted. Midge had been gone too long. He tried to convince himself that she had been delayed making her way out of the block, that she had had to hide from the men searching for them, but he knew he was ducking the truth. She had been taken; they had got her. He tried not to think what they would do to her to make her tell them where he was. He knew that he couldn't let that happen to her.

"All right," he said to the man in the cellar with him, "I'm going to get you out of there."

The man groaned his approval.

Vic placed the flash on the floor so that its light shone on the half-buried figure. He cleared away the rubble, then he picked up the length of lumber that would serve as a lever to raise the beam, shoved it underneath, tested it. Yes, it would work. In the next few seconds the man would be free. In the next few minutes, if the man was the watchman, he could be out of the cellar. If he wasn't the watchman, in the next few seconds, Vic knew, he could be dead. He took a deep breath and pressed down on the lever.

"Hey, mister!"

The cry was faint; it sounded miles away. He wasn't even sure that he had heard it at all, but he stopped straining on the lever and stood dead-still, listening. The cry was not repeated, and he knew it had been his imagination; in his desperation he had deluded himself into hearing what he wanted to hear. He set himself again to hoist the beam. Then his eyes and the man's eyes met, and he knew that it had not been his imagination. A boy had called out, the man had heard him, too. He pulled the lever from beneath the beam, threw it aside.

"Bud!" he called. "Bud!"

"Mister, hey, mister. Where are you?"

Bud's voice was moving closer. Vic swung the light in its direction. "Here, Bud, in the next cellar!"

"In the next cellar!" There was relief and triumph in Bud's voice. "You okay? The lady okay? I got my father here. . . ."

"Hold that light right where it is," Vic heard a man say. "It's coming through. I can see it! Maybe I can clear this away!"

Vic held the light steady. He could hear the sound of lumber being dragged aside, the clatter of bricks and plaster. Then a cascade of dust floated into the beam of the light and, as it settled, an empty window frame yawned down on him. Through the cloud of dust he could see the incredulous face of Bud's father, his hands extended through the window to him. He picked his way through the wrecked cellar. The hands reached down, grasped his wrists and then he felt himself being dragged to freedom.

Before he could get to his feet, Bud was saying, "Where's the lady, mister? What happened to the lady?"

"She got out."

From the cellar the man called out to them.

"Hey!" Bud's father said. "There's somebody else down there!"

"The watchman," Vic said.

Bud's father stooped down to look through the window and Vic put a hand on his shoulder. "We'll need the police to get him out. You go for the police. I'll stay here with him."

"You all right?" Bud's father said.

"I'm all right," Vic said. "If you'll get the cops here quick. . . ."

"Sure," Bud said, we'll get the cops! You stay here. We'll

get them!"

Vic watched them move away, then he flashed the light back through the window toward the man. "You heard, didn't you?" he said. "The cops will be here right away."

The man didn't answer.

As he moved away from the window, Vic heard nothing, saw no one. The night glow of the city outside that seeped into the project helped him thread his way through the piles of debris and the wrecking machinery. He reached the towering crane and ducked into the shelter of its shadow just in time. He saw a man not thirty feet away from him moving quickly but steathily in the direction of the cellar. For sure, Vic thought, he was one of them, coming to see what the hell was going on over here. As the man came abreast of the crane, Vic sidled around it, keeping the giant machine between them. Then, still using it as a shield, he crouched and ran toward the few houses that still stood on the other side of the block. He reached them, but just as he did, a slithering sound close by sent him flat up against the wall, holding his breath. It was minutes before he dared move again; when he did, a rat scurried between his feet.

He still carried the flashlight in his hand, but he knew he couldn't risk using it and he got rid of it. Feeling his way with outstretched hands, he groped into the nearest house, through its basement to the door that opened onto the sunken area and the street. It had been secured from the inside. He lifted the steel bar from its sockets and inched open the door. He glanced up and down the street; the near sidewalk was completely deserted. He stood there, momentarily defeated, knowing that he could not make a move without being instantly spotted.

Then came the shriek of sirens and in the next few moments three squad cars tore past his hideout, slowing down to a stop several doors away. They were followed and joined by an emergency truck, its revolving beacon shooting out red flares. He saw Bud's father lead the police into a house and soon the inside of the project was flooded with light and commotion. The crowd gathered quickly, streaming to the scene of disaster from all directions. The sidewalk and street were jammed. This was as big a crowd, Vic thought, as this particular attraction was likely to draw. He stepped up onto the sidewalk into the crowd and moved quickly through it, not too quickly, not noticeably in a hurry, just as fast as a man not interested in gawking at some unknown catastrophe might walk. Five minutes later he was standing on Third Avenue somewhere in the Eighties, nine or ten blocks away from the project. So far as he knew, he had not been spotted or followed. So far as he knew, for this moment, at any rate, he was in the clear.

Now, he thought, there was the problem of finding Midge. Somewhere among these millions of people, someplace in these hundreds of miles of streets was Midge. And he had no idea where to begin. And then, suddenly, something in his mind clicked and he knew exactly where he would at least begin to search for her. He looked up and down the avenue and saw a bar in the next block. He headed for it.

The look the bartender gave him when he entered made everyone else in the room turn to look at him. He caught a glimpse of himself in the mirror and realized that, of course, he looked like a man who had spent the last forty-eight hours in a filthy hole. Quickly, before the bartender could throw him out, he made for the men's room. He washed his face and hands, combed his hair and his beard with his fingers, using the remaining paper towels in the rack to wipe the grime off his clothing. Now, he thought, looking in the glass above the sink, he would not attract any more attention than any of the thousands of young men in New York who wore beards and levis, turtle-neck sweaters and casual jackets. He would be able, with any luck, to move about freely.

He found the phone booth in the back of the bar. There was still some change in his pocket, among it a dime. He dropped it in the slot and the number came to him instantly, his finger automatically spun the dial. That, he realized, was what was happening to him now. As he needed to remember things, they came back to him effortlessly.

The phone was answered after the first ring. The voice he heard was familiar to him; it was the voice that had always answered when he had checked in at this time of night. He identified himself. The voice responded with a cold matter-of-factness and no surprise. Vic might have been calling to check in every night for the past week.

"The McHenry Building," Vic said. "Do you know it?"

"Forty-second Street," the contact answered, "east of Eighth Avenue."

"Anything new there?" Vic asked.

"Not that I heard of. You think there might be?"

"Yes," Vic said, "I think there might be. I'm on my way there. I'll need help."

"Right," the contact said. "You'll get it."

He stood in front of the McHenry Building. Old and grubby and disreputable, it rose fourteen stories above a neighborhood that matched it for seediness and squalor. Many of its windows were lighted; here and there a whole floorful blazed out, so many that they gave him no clue. And he desperately needed a clue. Only the name of the building had flashed back to him. He didn't know where he had heard the name before, or under what circumstances, or why it was important. He only knew that it was important, that somewhere in the McHenry Building he might find Midge.

The ground floor was occupied by an open-all-night barbershop, an always open laundromat and by dry cleaners who were open twenty-four hours a day. The building's function was, obviously, to serve the night people. The rest of the street floor was taken over by a large honky-tonk place called a Fun-O-Rama. Inside it wooden ducks were being shot at, pinball machines played, a mechanical gypsy was telling fortunes, people weighed themselves, photographed themselves, watched minute movies. No one in the Fun-O-Rama seemed to pay any special attention to him; he saw no one he could tag as enemy, no one who gave him the signal that he was a friend.

As he walked past the shooting gallery, it occurred to him, and the thought tightened his shoulders, that the steady chorus of rifle shots would be a more than adequate cover for the noise of a gun fired at him.

He went into the lobby. One of the self-operating elevator's doors were opening. The passengers walked hurriedly toward the street, and the lobby for the moment was empty. Vic read the directory; no name on it meant anything to him. The elevator, still empty, stood with its doors open. Vic stepped inside it, poked a button. As the doors started to slide closed, a man ran through the lobby and into the elevator, grinning victoriously. Vic waited until the doors had almost closed, then squeezed through them back into the lobby. The man might not have been one of them, he might not have a gun, but he knew he must not risk being alone with anyone, in an elevator or anywhere else.

He found the stairs and climbed them to the second floor. There were bowling alleys there, about a dozen of them, most of them in action. There was a scattering of spectators. He walked the width of the room and back. Except for two lavatories and a small office with its door standing ajar, the bowling business occupied the entire floor. Covertly he examined the players, the spectators; no one responded. But once again his shoulders tightened; the constant din of balls crashing into pins would nicely swallow up a gun shot.

There was a fighters' gym on the next floor. Dozens of boxers, all shapes and sizes and colors, were sparring or jumping rope or punching bags under the critical eyes of handlers and friends. Vic moved quickly through the confusion, and the tightness in his shoulders spread into his belly. The machine gun rat-a-tat of the bags being punched would make the sound of a bullet unnoticeable. Quickly but carefully he checked the place and the people, then headed for the exit.

A hand grasped his arm from behind and swung him around. The man he faced was short and bulky, nattily dressed in Broadway's best, immaculately groomed. On one side of him stood a big, well-built boy in gloves and trunks, on the other side a young man in street clothes who might have been the fighter's older brother.

"Hey, man!" the bulky one shouted in Vic's face. "How much do you go?"

"Go?" Vic said.

"Weigh, man, weigh in at?"

The bulky one still had a firm grip on his arm. "About a hundred and eighty," Vic said.

"What I figured," the man said, "and you look in pretty good shape. How about you put on the gloves with my boy here for five, six rounds."

"Some other time," Vic said.

"There ain't some other time, man. The time is now!"

"Sorry," Vic said.

The fighter laid a glove on his right arm. "C'mon, man, give me a little workout. I'm lonely. No one here tonight for me to go with."

The fighter's big brother put a hand on his left arm. "C'mon, man, or are you chicken?"

"That's it," Vic said. He tried to shake the boys off him but, grinning, they tightened their grips on his arm. "You said it, I'm chicken."

A small crowd had begun to gather.

"No," the bulky one said, "you ain't chicken. I know chicken when I see it, and you ain't. C'mon, I'll get you some trunks and shoes."

"Okay," Vic said. "You get me trunks and shoes. Size ten." The boys released their grip and Vic stepped away. "First," he said, "I got to have a word with Manny. Be right back."

He hurried across the gym and into the corridor. No one followed him.

The next floor was in the process of being remodeled. In the glow of the light from the stairway landing he could see a half-laid dance floor; the place was empty.

He climbed the stairs to a landing that was larger than the one below, large enough to hold several beat-up leather sofas, a row of phone booths and a row of cigarette, candy and soft drink vending machines. At the moment it was deserted. Off it on four corridors were lines of recording studios. He glanced through the windows of the small, soundproofed rooms; in one a trio was recording, in another a combo. He saw nothing to keep him any longer on that floor.

He was stepping back into the lobby when he saw the man at the cigarette machine, fishing in his pocket for change, and Vic retreated quickly into the corridor. He had seen the man before; he had been, or had pretended to be, one of the onlookers down at the bowling alley. It could be, or might not be, a coincidence that now he was here, blocking Vic's path to the stairway. It would be impossible for him to get past the man unnoticed.

He heard the elevator stop, its doors open. A stout, breathless blonde rushed out of it and down a corridor. The man glanced at her, then stooped to gather up the cigarettes the machine was delivering, and in that moment Vic slid into the elevator.

The car was crowded. He looked at the button board. He saw that number eight had not been pressed, that no one meant to get off at that floor. He punched it.

At number six a woman got out, a delivery boy carrying a tray of sandwiches and coffee got on. The elevator was still filled, still a safe place. At number seven two women left. At number eight Vic took a step toward the opening doors. The man beside him moved toward them, too. Vic hesitated. Why, if the man had intended to alight at this floor, had he not pressed the button? Vic stepped out, then as the man walked past him into the lobby, he stepped back in again. At the ninth floor two couples moved toward the doors. Their departure would leave Vic alone in the cage with two men. Quickly he followed the couples.

The lettering on the frosted glass door they went through told Vic that this was Doc Miller's Health Club. He was in the reception room. Lettered arrows on the walls pointed the way to steam and massage rooms, to exercise rooms and a swimming pool, to the health cafeteria, the lounge and reading room. The reception room was half filled; the couples who had ridden up with him were standing at the desk. Across their shoulders he saw a woman in a white uniform come into the room from the cafeteria. She was a stout, pleasant-faced woman, hurrying about her business. Vic turned his back to her, hid his face. He knew her, he had reason never to forget her. She had driven him out to a lonely country road to be murdered. She had said her name was Polly Grant.

Now he knew that the name that had popped up out of his past was not merely a frantic hunch. Somewhere, sometime, he had known something important about the McHenry Building; now, for the first time, he felt certain that he was getting close to Midge.

He turned and over his shoulder he saw Polly Grant, striding purposefully, cross the reception room and go down one of the corridors. He started after her. When he reached the corridor, she was gone and for a moment he thought he had lost her. Then he caught a glimpse of the white uniform in a room beyond the hallway; she was headed for a door on its far side. The place was a lounge and reading room. By the time he got into it, Polly Grant had disappeared through the door.

There were no loungers in the room, only one reader. He was sitting in a chair that was between Vic and the far door, leafing through a magazine, and Vic knew that he was not going to let him get through that door. It was nothing he could put his finger on, but the warning was so strong and urgent that it sickened him. Somehow he knew, without a trace of doubt, that this broad-shouldered, surly-looking fellow was between him and Midge, and meant to keep it like that.

Halfway across the lounge he turned and looked back, knowing that he must find a path around the man guarding the door. He took one step and stopped again. Standing beside a library table beside the door Vic had just come through was a second man who had not been there a moment ago. He was a man whom he had seen twice before—once in the bowling alley, once in the lobby of the recording studios. He was still smoking the cigarette he had bought at the vending machine, but Vic knew that he would stop smoking it if he tried to go through that door.

There was a third door in the lounge, in the side wall to his right, and it was marked private. The thought came to him as he moved toward it that since it was marked as it was, it was probably kept locked. On the other hand, if it was always locked, why should anyone bother to mark it private? He grasped the knob, turned it, pushed. The door opened. As he closed it behind him, he turned the key in the lock. Then he turned to face the man who was rising from a chair behind the desk.

"Doctor Miller?" Vic asked pleasantly, moving toward the man behind the desk.

"No," the man said. "What's the matter? Can't you read?"

"Yes, I can and sometimes do," Vic said pleasantly, still moving toward the man behind the desk. "Why do you ask?"

"The door, it says private!"

"I wondered about that," Vic said, moving around the desk toward the man behind it. "Why does it say that?"

The man reached for the telephone. With his left fist Vic knocked down the man's extended hand. With his right fist he clipped him on the chin. The man fell back in his chair, his head rolled on his shoulders for a moment, then was still. Then Vic stepped to the only window in the small office and it pleased him immeasurably to see that it opened onto a fire escape.

Once again Midge felt the damp, cold cloth being lifted from her forehead. Once again she felt the hands that smelled of Jergen's Lotion press open her eyelid. She stared blankly up at the ceiling, not moving her eyes. She kept up the same rhythm of breathing that she had found herself doing when she regained consciousness. The hands left her face and she heard their owner grunt impatiently, angrily. There were quick footsteps, the sound of a door opening and then the gush of running water.

For the first time she dared open her eyes. The water was running behind a door that was half-closed. She sat up quickly, slid off the massage table on which she was lying, looked about her. She was in a small, windowless cubicle. On a table there was an array of bottles, lotions, rubbing alcohol, creams and oils. She caught a glimpse of herself in a mirror; she was wearing only a half slip and bra. She had been cleaned up, she saw; her face and hands, shoulders and arms had been washed. That was nice of them. She picked up the bottle of alcohol. It was large and heavy. She flattened herself against the wall beside the bathroom door. She raised the bottle above her head.

The water stopped running and the door was nudged wider open. Midge saw two hands that were carrying a wet towel, then a woman in a knee-length white smock stepped through the doorway. She stopped when she saw the empty massage table. She was turning toward Midge when the bottle broke on her head and she slumped to the floor.

Stepping over the woman, Midge went to a chair in the corner over which her clothes were draped. She slipped into her shoes, picked up her dress, threw it down again. The smock the woman was wearing might prove to be protective covering in this place, whatever it was. It took all her strength to wrestle the uniform off the woman, but in a minute she was buttoned into it and on her way to the door.

It opened onto a corridor lined with doors, indicating to Midge that she was in a cluster of massage rooms. The corridor itself was empty and she slipped into it. Before she had even decided which way to turn, the door opposite her opened and an elderly woman stepped out. Her hair was done up in curlers; her face gleamed with cream and the rest of her was swathed in Turkish towels. She smiled at Midge.

"Which way to the showers, dearie?" she said.

Midge pointed to the left.

"Thank you."

The woman went to the left, Midge to the right. Her heart was pounding; it was all she could do to keep from breaking into a wild dash and trusting to luck that she would find her way to safety. She thought that she should have asked the woman who needed a shower for help, then decided no, she hadn't looked as if she could be of any help. At a turning in the hallway Midge heard a man's voice; it was a voice that she had heard before and it drew her up short.

Back in the massage room, while she had been feigning unconsciousness, this man had come into the room. He had spoken to the woman attendant, told her to use cold towels to get the girl on her feet and in shape to talk. His tone told Midge he would not waste any time being gentle with her; he was in a hurry to find out where she and the man they thought was Vic Jacoby had been hiding.

The voice came closer. Beside her was a pair of double doors that opened onto an unlit room. Before she darted into it, she was able to see from the corridor lights that it was some sort of storage room. She had caught sight of piled-up furniture, boxes, cartons, crates.

She pressed her ear against the door and heard the man's voice and his footsteps as he passed only a few inches from her. Then, at the other end of the storage room she heard a door softly open, softly close. She saw a tall figure grope its way through the clutter of furniture and crates. She backed into a corner against the wall, crouched down against it. The sound of steps came closer. The man was standing at the door now, right beside her. He inched open the door and a streak of light fell across his face. In her relief and surprise she almost shouted his name.

She got to her feet and whispered, "Larry, I'm here."

His arms found her and held her close to him. "Midge. Midge, are you all right?"

"Yes. Don't go out that door, Larry. That's where they are."

"We'll go back the way I came," he said. "We'll get out of this, Midge."

They groped their way through the furniture and stacks of folding chairs to a door at the other side. Outside it Vic knew was a hallway leading to a flight of stairs. He eased the door open; the hall was empty.

He took Midge's hand and they ran toward the steps. They saw no one, heard no one. They had gone down one flight, then halfway down another and he knew that now they were well on their way to safety. Then he saw Midge turn, look back up the stairs and stifle the scream that was rising in her lips. He saw the shadow of the man, gun in hand, coming down toward them. He knew they couldn't reach the next landing.

Then the man followed his shadow around the curve in the staircase. He looked down at them and slipped his gun into the shoulder holster, and he smiled. It was a grim smile, but a friendly one.

"It's Tom Bates," Vic said to Midge.

"Oh," Midge said. "Tom Bates."

"I've had a hell of a time catching up to you," Tom said. "What do you say we go someplace where we can talk."

"There's a fire escape," Vic said. "We can get out that way."

"I have a better way," Tom Bates said. "Up the freight elevator and across the roof to the next building."

"That," Vic said, "does sound like a better way."

"Follow me," Tom Bates said.

"Gladly," Vic said.

"With pleasure," Midge said.

Tom went ahead of them to the foot of that flight of steps, opened a door there and then beckoned to them. They followed him down a silent, darkened corridor to its end. Although they walked stealthily, their footsteps seemed to ring out and echo in the silence. Tom stopped before large elevator doors, pushed a button and in a moment they opened and the empty car stood in front of them. They slipped into it and the cage started grumbling upward.

Midge collapsed against Vic and he could feel the tremors that were racking her body and he held her tightly. Tom Bates glanced at them, then turned to face the wall that was sliding down past them. A number nine appeared on the wall and they crept above it toward the floor numbered ten. The elevator was droning up at a snail's pace, cables protesting noisily every inch of the way. Vic wondered how many floors the building had, and then remembered that down on the street he had counted fourteen rows of windows.

"Almost there, Midge," he said. "Thanks to Tom. And incidentally, Tom, thanks."

"Don't mention it," Tom said, and grinned. "The least I could do for an old buddy."

Those words, spoken casually, flippantly, by Tom, threw Vic's mind back again into the past. He was reliving those two hours he had spent on the road between Cadaqués and Figueras, two lost hours when he thought he had been drugged. Now he knew that he had not been drugged; during those hours something had happened that he had rejected, something that he did not want to remember.

He held Midge close, but he was no longer in a decrepit old freight elevator with her and his old buddy Tom Bates, climbing to their escape. He was back in Spain; it was the afternoon before Enid and Gerald and Nicole had died in the flaming car.

He had left Cadaqués and pulled off the road at sunset beside a small cement block that read Figueras . . . 25 kms. The agent in the bar, posing as a tourist, had given him the code word, violets. He had mentioned Figueras, and the number twenty-five. This was the spot designated for a rendezvous.

He waited. The sunset faded; the flaming sky turned purple and a cold breeze swept down from the mountains. He turned up the collar of his jacket and looked at his watch. It had been more than an hour since he had parked beside the kilometer marker.

Then, a moment later, he saw the headlights brush across the silver leaves of the olive grove, and then he saw the outline of a car as it followed the lights around a bend in the road and speeded toward him. It passed, but then stopped, and the tall figure of one of his superiors, a man named Darrow, was coming toward him. Vic waited for him, and he saw that his face was grim.

"Something has gone wrong," he said.

"Yes, a little something has gone wrong," Darrow said.

"I thought we'd done a hell of a good job."

"No, the whole operation is a washout, a fiasco, a complete bust."

Vic stared at him incredulously. "What went wrong?"

"Tom Bates went wrong."

"Tom Bates," he said. "No, I don't believe it."

"Yes," Darrow said. He lit a cigarette. He expelled a stream of smoke, shook out the match. "Our side isn't the only side Tom is working for."

"Tom went over," Vic said. "I still can't believe it."

"You'd better believe it. Tommy is now earning two salaries, one from them and one from us. Money can do that to some people. It did it to Tommy."

"So now they know who we are," Vic said. "They'll be gunning for us."

"That's right."

"Who knows about this? Enid? Gerald?"

"No, only I know. And now you know."

"I see," Vic said. "You're here to tell me that we should look after Tom."

"Yes," Darrow said. "Would you mind doing that?"

"I will hate doing that to Tom," Vic said, "but it's either him or us."

"Exactly," Darrow said. "And you'll see to it immediately?"

"At once," Vic said.

He put his car in gear, his superior started walking back to his car. Vic swung into a U-turn that edged a deep gorge. A Mercedes roared past him, going at such a recklessly insane speed that it made Vic pull off to the side of the road to watch it. Across the gorge he saw Darrow, about to get into his car, turn to face the Mercedes. He heard the fusillade of shots and in the glare of the Mercedes' headlights he saw Darrow pitch forward and fall into the path of the onrushing car. He saw the car jolt as it passed over his body. Now only he knew about Tom Bates.

In Figueras he put in the phone call to Cala Brava. Gerald told him that Tom Bates had left for Barcelona; he was catching the night plane to New York. Vic told him that they must see to it that Tom did not get on that plane. Tom had defected; he was a double agent.

The elevator wheezed to a stop at the top floor of the McHenry Building. As its doors creaked open, Tom drew his gun from its holster. He stepped cautiously out onto the landing, looked around, then turned back to Midge and Vic.

"Okay," he said. He crossed the landing to the stairs that led to the roof and looked up them. "Also okay," he said. "The coast seems clear. Won't you join me?" He made a mock, elaborate gesture inviting Midge and Vic to precede him up the stairs. "Ladies and gentlemen first," he said.

"Appreciate that, Tom," Vic said, "but you go first. You have the gun. And there may be someone who is no friend of ours up there on the roof."

"Could be," Tom said. "How like them to have someone up there."

He started up the stairs. Midge moved to follow him, but

Vic stepped into the stairway ahead of her. The three of them, Tom with the gun, then Vic, then Midge, climbed the stairs to the steel door at the top. Tom opened it, stepped out onto the roof, looked around.

"The coast," he said, "remains clear."

With his gun hand he again made the mock gesture, inviting them to come out onto the roof. Again they accepted the invitation. Vic stepped over the threshold, then Midge. Tom closed the door and turned to them.

"Sorry about this," he said.

As his gun hand was rising, Vic hit him. The blow caught him on the point of his chin, his chin snapped back and as he fell, the gun dropped from his hand. Vic scooped it up. He aimed it at Tom, then thought of Midge there beside him and he did not pull the trigger. Tom was out, he could be taken care of later. He put his arm around Midge and helped her across the roof to the adjacent building.

"Sorry about that," he said, "but it's my gun. He borrowed it and never returned it."

He kept his arm around her as they went down the stairs from the roof, and in a moment they were in another elevator that seemed warm and cozy and friendly. It was carrying them to safety; they were going to be safe at last. He smiled at Midge; she managed a smile back, a wan, bewildered smile.

"There's so much to explain," he said. "But do you mind if first I tell you that I wouldn't mind spending the rest of my life in a dirty cellar with you?"

"Huh?" she said.

"Let me put it this way," he said. "I love you."

"Love me?"

"And I want you to be my wife," he said. "Will you

marry me?"

"Oh, yes!" she said. "But, Larry, I have to tell you. . . . I'm afraid I'm still a little bit in love with Vic Jacoby. I'm afraid that maybe I always will be."

"You're still in love with Vic Jacoby," he said.

"Yes," she said.

"Midge," he said, "I have news for you."